Dear Reader,

It is very difficult for me to write about myself, and especially *The Outsiders*, which was written at a horrendous time in my life, was published by a series of mind-boggling synchronicities, and has gone further than any author dared dream. But I'll give it a shot.

I wrote *The Outsiders* when I was sixteen years old. Actually I began it when I was fifteen, as a short story about a boy who was beaten up on his way home from the movies.

But I didn't just write *The Outsiders*, I lived it. Looking back, I realize how important it was to me to have another life at that time. To be someone else. To deal with problems I had to face, and write my way to some sort of understanding and coping. This is all in hindsight. At the time, I was mad about the social situation in my high school. I desperately wanted something to read that dealt realistically with teen-age life.

I knew I was going to be a writer. I love to write. I began in grade school, because I loved to read, and liked the idea of making stories happen the way I wanted them to. By the time I was in high school I had been practicing for years. So I was both elated and not surprised when I received my publishing contract on the day I graduated from high school.

The Outsiders has taken me many places I never dreamed of going. It introduced me to people I would never otherwise have met. Although the names Patrick Swayze, Tom Cruise, Matt Dillon, Rob Lowe, C. Thomas Howell, Emilio Estevez, and Ralph Macchio are familiar to most people, and conjure visions of movie stars and glamour, I remember a group of sweet, goofy, incredibly talented and at the same time incredibly normal teen-age boys. I was involved in every aspect of filming the movie version of *The Outsiders*, and the memory I cherish most is of hanging out with "my boys."

I owe Francis Coppola a debt of thanks. Not only for the respect, kindness, and friendship I personally received from him, but for the fact that he made the movie for the fans of the book. He shot a faithful adaptation, consulting me for everything from locations to wardrobe, but it was the fans of the book he wanted to please. And as far as I know, he is the only director to go back and assemble a more complete movie (*The Outsiders, The Complete Novel* DVD) because those fans asked him to.

Fans. I receive letters from every state, from dozens of foreign countries. From twelve-year-olds and forty-year-olds. From convicts and policemen, teachers, social workers, and of course, kids. Kids who are living lives like those in *The Outsiders*. Kids who can't imagine living lives like those in *The Outsiders*. Kids who read all the time. Ones who never before finished a book.

The letters saying "I loved the book" are good, the ones that say "I never liked to read before, and now I read all the time" are better, but the ones that say "*The Outsiders* changed my life" and "I read it fifteen years ago and I realize how much it has influenced my life choices" frankly scare me. Who am I to change anyone's life? I guess the best reply is "It's the book, not the author" and "It's the message, not the messenger." A lot of the time I feel that *The Outsiders* was meant to be written, and I was chosen to write it. It's certainly done more good than anything I could accomplish on a personal level.

If this sounds like I am overwhelmed by the decades of incredible response to what began as a short story I started when I was fifteen years old, well, I guess that's the truth.

Stay Gold.

S. E. Hinton

THE
OUTSIDERS

S. E. HINTON

PENGUIN BOOKS

PENGUIN BOOKS
An imprint of Penguin Random House LLC, New York

First published in the United States of America by The Viking Press, 1967
Published by Puffin Books, a division of Penguin Young Readers Group, 1997
This edition published by Speak, an imprint of Penguin Group (USA) Inc., 2006, 2012

Penguin & colophon are registered trademarks of Penguin Books Limited.

Visit us online at penguinrandomhouse.com.

THE LIBRARY OF CONGRESS HAS CATALOGED THE VIKING EDITION
UNDER CATALOG CARD NUMBER: 67-13606

Platinum Edition ISBN 9780142407332

Printed in the United States of America

43

BOOKS BY S. E. HINTON

Big David, Little David
Hawke's Harbor
The Outsiders
The Puppy Sister
Rumble Fish
Some of Tim's Stories
Tex
That Was Then, This Is Now

For Jimmy

THE
OUTSIDERS

Chapter 1

WHEN I STEPPED out into the bright sunlight from the darkness of the movie house, I had only two things on my mind: Paul Newman and a ride home. I was wishing I looked like Paul Newman —he looks tough and I don't—but I guess my own looks aren't so bad. I have light-brown, almost-red hair and greenish-gray eyes. I wish they were more gray, because I hate most guys that have green eyes, but I have to be content with what I have. My hair is longer than a lot of boys wear theirs, squared off in back and long at the front and sides, but I am a greaser and most of my neighborhood rarely bothers to get a haircut. Besides, I look better with long hair.

I had a long walk home and no company, but I usually lone it anyway, for no reason except that I like to watch movies undisturbed so I can get into them and live them with the actors. When I see a movie with someone it's kind of uncomfortable, like having someone read your book over your shoulder. I'm different that way. I mean, my second-oldest brother, Soda, who is sixteen-going-on-seventeen, never cracks a book at all, and my oldest brother, Darrel, who we call Darry, works too long and hard to be interested in a story or drawing a picture, so I'm not like them. And nobody in our gang digs movies and books the way I do. For a while there, I thought I was the only person in the world that did. So I loned it.

Soda tries to understand, at least, which is more than Darry does. But then, Soda is different from anybody; he understands everything, almost. Like he's never hollering at me all the time the way Darry is, or treating me as if I was six instead of fourteen. I love Soda more than I've ever loved anyone, even Mom and Dad. He's always happy-go-lucky and grinning, while Darry's hard and firm and rarely grins at all. But then, Darry's gone through a lot in his twenty years, grown up too fast. Sodapop'll never grow up at all. I don't know which way's the best. I'll find out one of these days.

Anyway, I went on walking home, thinking about the movie, and then suddenly wishing I had some company. Greasers can't walk alone too much or they'll get jumped, or someone will come by and scream "Greaser!" at them, which doesn't make you feel too hot, if you know what I mean. We get jumped by the Socs. I'm not sure how you spell it, but it's the abbreviation for the Socials, the jet set, the West-side rich kids. It's like the term "greaser," which is used to class all us boys on the East Side.

We're poorer than the Socs and the middle class. I reckon we're wilder, too. Not like the Socs, who jump greasers and wreck houses and throw beer blasts for kicks, and get editorials in the paper for being a public disgrace one day and an asset to society the next. Greasers are almost like hoods; we steal things and drive old souped-up cars and hold up gas stations and have a gang fight once in a while. I don't mean I do things like that. Darry would kill me if I got into trouble with the police. Since Mom and Dad were killed in an auto wreck, the three of us get to stay together only as long as we behave. So Soda and I stay out of trouble as much as we can, and we're careful not to get caught when we can't. I only mean that most greasers do things like that, just like we wear our hair long and dress in blue jeans and T-shirts, or leave our shirttails out and wear leather jackets and tennis shoes or boots. I'm not saying that either Socs or greasers are better; that's just the way things are.

I could have waited to go to the movies until Darry or Sodapop got off work. They would have gone with me, or driven me there, or walked along, although Soda just can't sit still long enough to enjoy a movie and they bore Darry to death. Darry thinks his life is enough without inspecting other people's. Or I could have gotten one of the gang to come along, one of the four boys Darry and Soda and I have grown up with and consider family. We're almost as close as brothers; when you grow up in a tight-knit neighborhood like ours you get to know each other real well. If I had thought about it, I could have called Darry and he would have come by on his way home and picked me up, or Two-Bit Mathews—one of our gang—would have come to get me in his car if I had asked him, but sometimes I just don't use my head. It drives my brother Darry nuts when I do stuff like that, 'cause I'm supposed to be smart; I make good grades and have a high IQ and everything, but I don't use my head. Besides, I like walking.

I about decided I didn't like it so much, though, when I spotted that red Corvair trailing me. I was almost two blocks from home then, so I started walking a little faster. I had never been jumped, but I had seen Johnny after four Socs got hold of him, and it wasn't pretty. Johnny was scared of his own shadow after that. Johnny was sixteen then.

I knew it wasn't any use though—the fast walking, I mean—even before the Corvair pulled up beside me and five Socs got out. I got pretty scared—I'm kind of small for fourteen even though I have a good build, and those guys were bigger than me. I automatically hitched my thumbs in my jeans and slouched, wondering if I could get away if I made a break for it. I remembered Johnny—his face all cut up and bruised, and I remembered how he had cried when we found him, half-conscious, in the corner lot. Johnny had it awful rough at home—it took a lot to make him cry.

I was sweating something fierce, although I was cold. I could feel my palms getting clammy and the perspiration running down my back. I get like that when I'm real scared. I glanced around for a pop bottle or a stick or something—Steve Randle, Soda's best buddy, had once held off four guys with a busted pop bottle—but there was nothing. So I stood there like a bump on a log while they surrounded me. I don't use my head. They walked around slowly, silently, smiling.

"Hey, grease," one said in an over-friendly voice. "We're gonna do you a favor, greaser. We're gonna cut all that long greasy hair off."

He had on a madras shirt. I can still see it. Blue madras. One of them laughed, then cussed me out in a low voice. I couldn't think of anything to say. There just isn't a whole lot you can say while waiting to get mugged, so I kept my mouth shut.

"Need a haircut, greaser?" The medium-sized blond pulled a knife out of his back pocket and flipped the blade open.

I finally thought of something to say. "No." I was backing up, away from that knife. Of course I backed right into one of them. They had me down in a second. They had my arms and legs pinned down and one of them was sitting on my chest with his knees on my elbows, and if you don't think that hurts, you're crazy. I could smell English Leather shaving lotion and stale tobacco, and I wondered foolishly if I would suffocate before they did anything. I was scared so bad I was wishing I would. I fought to get loose, and almost did for a second; then they tightened up on me and the one on my chest slugged me a couple of times. So I lay still, swearing at them between gasps. A blade was held against my throat.

"How'd you like that haircut to begin just below the chin?"

It occurred to me then that they could kill me. I went wild. I started screaming for Soda, Darry, anyone. Someone put his hand over my mouth, and I bit it as hard as I could, tasting the blood running through my teeth. I heard a muttered curse and got slugged again, and they were stuffing a handkerchief in my mouth. One of them kept saying, "Shut him up, for Pete's sake, shut him up!"

Then there were shouts and the pounding of feet, and the Socs jumped up and left me lying there, gasping. I lay there and wondered what in the world was happening—people were jumping over me and running by me and I was too dazed to figure it out. Then someone had me under the armpits and was hauling me to my feet. It was Darry.

"Are you all right, Ponyboy?"

He was shaking me and I wished he'd stop. I was dizzy enough anyway. I could tell it was Darry though—partly because of the voice and partly because Darry's always rough with me without meaning to be.

"I'm okay. Quit shaking me, Darry, I'm okay."

He stopped instantly. "I'm sorry."

He wasn't really. Darry isn't ever sorry for anything he does. It seems funny to me that he should look just exactly like my father and act exactly the opposite from him. My father was only forty when he died and he looked twenty-five and a lot of people thought Darry and Dad were brothers instead of father and son. But they only looked alike—my father was never rough with anyone without meaning to be.

Darry is six-feet-two, and broad-shouldered and muscular. He has dark-brown hair that kicks out in front and a slight cowlick in the back—just like Dad's—but Darry's eyes are his own. He's got eyes that are like two pieces of pale blue-green ice. They've got a determined set to them, like the rest of him. He looks older than twenty—tough, cool, and smart. He would be real handsome if his eyes weren't so cold. He doesn't understand anything that is not plain hard fact. But he uses his head.

I sat down again, rubbing my cheek where I'd been slugged the most.

Darry jammed his fists in his pockets. "They didn't hurt you too bad, did they?"

They did. I was smarting and aching and my chest was sore and I was so nervous my hands were shaking and I wanted to start bawling, but you just don't say that to Darry.

"I'm okay."

Sodapop came loping back. By then I had figured that all the noise I had heard was the gang coming to rescue me. He dropped down beside me, examining my head.

"You got cut up a little, huh, Ponyboy?"

I only looked at him blankly. "I did?"

He pulled out a handkerchief, wet the end of it with his tongue, and pressed it gently against the side of my head. "You're bleedin' like a stuck pig."

"I am?"

"Look!" He showed me the handkerchief, reddened as if by magic. "Did they pull a blade on you?"

I remembered the voice: "Need a haircut, greaser?" The blade must have slipped while he was trying to shut me up. "Yeah."

Soda is handsomer than anyone else I know. Not like Darry—Soda's movie-star kind of handsome, the kind that people stop on the street to watch go by. He's not as tall as Darry, and he's a little slimmer, but he has a finely drawn, sensitive face that somehow manages to be reckless and thoughtful at the same time. He's got dark-gold hair that he combs back—long and silky and straight—and in the summer the sun bleaches it to a shining wheat-gold. His eyes are dark brown—lively, dancing, recklessly laughing eyes that can be gentle and sympathetic one moment and blazing with anger the next. He has Dad's eyes, but Soda is one of a kind. He can get drunk in a drag race or dancing without ever getting near alcohol. In our neighborhood it's rare to find a kid who doesn't drink once in a while. But Soda never touches a drop—he doesn't need to. He gets drunk on just plain living. And he understands everybody.

He looked at me more closely. I looked away hurriedly, because, if you want to know the truth, I was starting to bawl. I knew I was as white as I felt and I was shaking like a leaf.

Soda just put his hand on my shoulder. "Easy, Ponyboy. They ain't gonna hurt you no more."

"I know," I said, but the ground began to blur and I felt hot tears running down my cheeks. I brushed them away impatiently. "I'm just a little spooked, that's all." I drew a quivering breath and quit crying. You just don't cry in front of Darry. Not unless you're hurt like Johnny had been that day we found him in the vacant lot. Compared to Johnny I wasn't hurt at all.

Soda rubbed my hair. "You're an okay kid, Pony."

I had to grin at him—Soda can make you grin no matter what. I guess it's because he's always grinning so much himself. "You're crazy, Soda, out of your mind."

Darry looked as if he'd like to knock our heads together. "You're both nuts."

Soda merely cocked one eyebrow, a trick he'd picked up from Two-Bit. "It seems to run in this family."

Darry stared at him for a second, then cracked a grin. Sodapop isn't afraid of him like everyone else and enjoys teasing him. I'd just as soon tease a full-grown grizzly; but for some reason, Darry seems to like being teased by Soda.

Our gang had chased the Socs to their car and heaved rocks at them. They came running toward us now—four lean, hard guys. They were all as tough as nails and looked it. I had grown up with them, and they accepted me, even though I was younger, because I was Darry and Soda's kid brother and I kept my mouth shut good.

Steve Randle was seventeen, tall and lean, with thick greasy hair he kept combed in complicated swirls. He was cocky, smart, and Soda's best buddy since grade school. Steve's specialty was cars. He could lift a hubcap quicker and more quietly than anyone in the neighborhood, but he also knew cars upside-down and backward, and he could drive anything on wheels. He and Soda worked at the same gas station—Steve part time and Soda full time—and their station got more customers than any other in town. Whether that was because Steve was so good with cars or because Soda attracted girls like honey draws flies, I couldn't tell you. I liked Steve only because he was Soda's best friend. He didn't like me—he thought I was a tagalong and a kid; Soda always took me with them when they went places if they weren't taking girls, and that bugged Steve. It wasn't my fault; Soda always asked me, I didn't ask him. Soda doesn't think I'm a kid.

Two-Bit Mathews was the oldest of the gang and the wisecracker of the bunch. He was about six feet tall, stocky in build, and very proud of his long rusty-colored sideburns. He had gray eyes and a wide grin, and he couldn't stop making funny remarks to save his life. You couldn't shut up that guy; he always had to get his two-bits worth in. Hence his name. Even his teachers forgot his real name was Keith, and we hardly remembered he had one. Life was one big joke to Two-Bit. He was famous for shoplifting and his black-handled switchblade (which he couldn't have acquired without his first talent), and he was always smarting off to the cops. He really couldn't help it. Everything he said was so irresistibly funny that he just had to let the police in on it to brighten up their dull lives. (That's the way he explained it to me.) He liked fights, blondes, and for some unfathomable reason, school. He was still a junior at eighteen and a half and he never learned anything. He just went for kicks. I liked him real well because he kept us laughing at ourselves as well as at other things. He reminded me of Will Rogers—maybe it was the grin.

If I had to pick the real character of the gang, it would be Dallas Winston—Dally. I used to like to draw his picture when he was in a dangerous mood, for then I could get his personality down in a few lines. He had an elfish face, with high cheekbones and a pointed chin, small, sharp animal teeth, and ears like a lynx. His hair was almost white it was so blond, and he didn't like haircuts, or hair oil either, so it fell over his forehead in wisps and kicked out in the back in tufts and curled behind his ears and along the nape of his neck. His eyes were blue, blazing ice, cold with a hatred of the whole world. Dally had spent three years on the wild side of New York and had been arrested at the age of ten. He was tougher than the rest of us—tougher, colder, meaner. The shade of difference that separates a greaser from a hood wasn't present in Dally. He was as wild as the boys in the downtown outfits, like Tim Shepard's gang.

In New York, Dally blew off steam in gang fights, but here, organized gangs are rarities—there are just small bunches of friends who stick together, and the warfare is between the social classes. A rumble, when it's called, is usually born of a grudge fight, and the opponents just happen to bring their friends along. Oh, there are a few named gangs around, like the River Kings and the Tiber Street Tigers, but here in the Southwest there's no gang rivalry. So Dally, even though he could get into a good fight sometimes, had no specific thing to hate. No rival gang. Only Socs. And you can't win against them no matter how hard you try, because they've got all the breaks and even whipping them isn't going to change that fact. Maybe that was why Dallas was so bitter.

He had quite a reputation. They have a file on him down at the police station. He had been arrested, he got drunk, he rode in rodeos, lied, cheated, stole, rolled drunks, jumped small kids—he did everything. I didn't like him, but he was smart and you had to respect him.

Johnny Cade was last and least. If you can picture a little dark puppy that has been kicked too many times and is lost in a crowd of strangers, you'll have Johnny. He was the youngest, next to me, smaller than the rest, with a slight build. He had big black eyes in a dark tanned face; his hair was jet-black and heavily greased and combed to the side, but it was so long that it fell in shaggy bangs across his forehead. He had a nervous, suspicious look in his eyes, and that beating he got from the Socs didn't help matters. He was the gang's pet, everyone's kid brother. His father was always beating him up, and his mother ignored him, except when she was hacked off at something, and then you could hear her yelling at him clear down at our house. I think he hated that worse than getting whipped. He would have run away a million times if we hadn't been there. If it hadn't been for the gang, Johnny would never have known what love and affection are.

I wiped my eyes hurriedly. "Didya catch 'em?"

"Nup. They got away this time, the dirty . . ." Two-Bit went on cheerfully, calling the Socs every name he could think of or make up.

"The kid's okay?"

"I'm okay." I tried to think of something to say. I'm usually pretty quiet around people, even the gang. I changed the subject. "I didn't know you were out of the cooler yet, Dally."

"Good behavior. Got off early." Dallas lit a cigarette and handed it to Johnny. Everyone sat down to have a smoke and relax. A smoke always lessens the tension. I had quit trembling and my color was back. The cigarette was calming me down. Two-Bit cocked an eyebrow. "Nice-lookin' bruise you got there, kid."

I touched my cheek gingerly. "Really?"

Two-Bit nodded sagely. "Nice cut, too. Makes you look tough."

Tough and *tuff* are two different words. *Tough* is the same as rough; *tuff* means cool, sharp—like a tuff-looking Mustang or a tuff record. In our neighborhood both are compliments.

Steve flicked his ashes at me. "What were you doin', walkin' by your lonesome?" Leave it to good old Steve to bring up something like that.

"I was comin' home from the movies. I didn't think . . ."

"You don't ever think," Darry broke in, "not at home or anywhere when it counts. You must think at school, with all those good grades you bring home, and you've always got your nose in a book, but do you ever use your head for common sense? No sirree, bub. And if you did have to go by yourself, you should have carried a blade."

I just stared at the hole in the toe of my tennis shoe. Me and Darry just didn't dig each other. I never could please him. He would have hollered at me for carrying a blade if I *had* carried one. If I brought home B's, he wanted A's, and if I got A's, he wanted to make sure they stayed A's. If I was playing football, I should be in studying, and if I was reading, I should be out playing football. He never hollered at Sodapop—not even when Soda dropped out of school or got tickets for speeding. He just hollered at me.

Soda was glaring at him. "Leave my kid brother alone, you hear? It ain't his fault he likes to go to the movies, and it ain't his fault the Socs like to jump us, and if he had been carrying a blade it would have been a good excuse to cut him to ribbons."

Soda always takes up for me.

Darry said impatiently, "When I want my kid brother to tell me what to do with my other kid brother, I'll ask you— kid brother." But he laid off me. He always does when Sodapop tells him to. Most of the time.

"Next time get one of us to go with you, Ponyboy," Two-Bit said. "Any of us will."

"Speakin' of movies"—Dally yawned, flipping away his cigarette butt—"I'm walkin' over to the Nightly Double tomorrow night. Anybody want to come and hunt some action?"

Steve shook his head. "Me and Soda are pickin' up Evie and Sandy for the game."

He didn't need to look at me the way he did right then. I wasn't going to ask if I could come. I'd never tell Soda, because he really likes Steve a lot, but sometimes I can't stand Steve Randle. I mean it. Sometimes I hate him.

Darry sighed, just like I knew he would. Darry never had time to do anything anymore. "I'm working tomorrow night."

Dally looked at the rest of us. "How about y'all? Two-Bit? Johnnycake, you and Pony wanta come?"

"Me and Johnny'll come," I said. I knew Johnny wouldn't open his mouth unless he was forced to. "Okay, Darry?"

"Yeah, since it ain't a school night." Darry was real good about letting me go places on the weekends. On school nights I could hardly leave the house.

"I was plannin' on getting boozed up tomorrow night," Two-Bit said. "If I don't, I'll walk over and find y'all."

Steve was looking at Dally's hand. His ring, which he had rolled a drunk senior to get, was back on his finger. "You break up with Sylvia again?"

"Yeah, and this time it's for good. That little broad was two-timin' me again while I was in jail."

I thought of Sylvia and Evie and Sandy and Two-Bit's many blondes. They were the only kind of girls that would look at us, I thought. Tough, loud girls who wore too much eye makeup and giggled and swore too much. I liked

Soda's girl Sandy just fine, though. Her hair was natural blond and her laugh was soft, like her china-blue eyes. She didn't have a real good home or anything and was our kind—greaser—but she was a real nice girl. Still, lots of times I wondered what other girls were like. The girls who were bright-eyed and had their dresses a decent length and acted as if they'd like to spit on us if given a chance. Some were afraid of us, and remembering Dallas Winston, I didn't blame them. But most looked at us like we were dirt—gave us the same kind of look that the Socs did when they came by in their Mustangs and Corvairs and yelled "Grease!" at us. I wondered about them. The girls, I mean . . . Did they cry when their boys were arrested, like Evie did when Steve got hauled in, or did they run out on them the way Sylvia did Dallas? But maybe their boys didn't get arrested or beaten up or busted up in rodeos.

I was still thinking about it while I was doing my homework that night. I had to read *Great Expectations* for English, and that kid Pip, he reminded me of us—the way he felt marked lousy because he wasn't a gentleman or anything, and the way that girl kept looking down on him. That happened to me once. One time in biology I had to dissect a worm, and the razor wouldn't cut, so I used my switchblade. The minute I flicked it out—I forgot what I was doing or I would never have done it—this girl right beside me kind of gasped, and said, "They are right. You are a hood." That didn't make me feel so hot. There were a lot of Socs in that class—I get put into A classes because I'm supposed to be smart—and most of them thought it was pretty funny. I didn't, though. She was a cute girl. She looked real good in yellow.

We deserve a lot of our trouble, I thought. Dallas deserves everything he gets, and should get worse, if you want the truth. And Two-Bit—he doesn't really want or need half the things he swipes from stores. He just thinks it's fun to swipe everything that isn't nailed down. I can understand why Sodapop and Steve get into drag races and fights so much, though—both of them have too much energy, too much feeling, with no way to blow it off.

"Rub harder, Soda," I heard Darry mumbling. "You're gonna put me to sleep."

I looked through the door. Sodapop was giving Darry a back-rub. Darry is always pulling muscles; he roofs houses and he's always trying to carry two bundles of roofing up the ladder. I knew Soda would put him to sleep, because Soda can put about anyone out when he sets his head to it. He thought Darry worked too hard anyway. I did, too.

Darry didn't deserve to work like an old man when he was only twenty. He had been a real popular guy in school; he was captain of the football team and he had been voted Boy of the Year. But we just didn't have the money for him to go to college, even with the athletic scholarship he won. And now he didn't have time between jobs to even think about college. So he never went anywhere and never did anything anymore, except work out at gyms and go skiing with some old friends of his sometimes.

I rubbed my cheek where it had turned purple. I had looked in the mirror, and it did make me look tough. But Darry had made me put a Band-Aid on the cut.

I remembered how awful Johnny had looked when he got beaten up. I had just as much right to use the streets as the Socs did, and Johnny had never hurt them. Why did the Socs hate us so much? We left them alone. I nearly went to sleep over my homework trying to figure it out.

Sodapop, who had jumped into bed by this time, yelled sleepily for me to turn off the light and get to bed. When I finished the chapter I was on, I did.

Lying beside Soda, staring at the wall, I kept remembering the faces of the Socs as they surrounded me, that blue madras shirt the blond was wearing, and I could still hear a thick voice: "Need a haircut, greaser?" I shivered.

"You cold, Ponyboy?"

"A little," I lied. Soda threw one arm across my neck. He mumbled something drowsily. "Listen, kiddo, when Darry hollers at you . . . he don't mean nothin'. He's just got more worries than somebody his age ought to. Don't take him serious . . . you dig, Pony? Don't let him bug you. He's really proud of you 'cause you're so brainy. It's just because you're the baby—I mean, he loves you a lot. Savvy?"

"Sure," I said, trying for Soda's sake to keep the sarcasm out of my voice.

"Soda?"

"Yeah?"

"How come you dropped out?" I never have gotten over that. I could hardly stand it when he left school.

"'Cause I'm dumb. The only things I was passing anyway were auto mechanics and gym."

"You're not dumb."

"Yeah, I am. Shut up and I'll tell you something. Don't tell Darry, though."

"Okay."

"I think I'm gonna marry Sandy. After she gets out of

school and I get a better job and everything. I might wait till you get out of school, though. So I can still help Darry with the bills and stuff."

"Tuff enough. Wait till I get out, though, so you can keep Darry off my back."

"Don't be like that, kid. I told you he don't mean half of what he says . . ."

"You in love with Sandy? What's it like?"

"Hhhmmm." He sighed happily. "It's real nice."

In a moment his breathing was light and regular. I turned my head to look at him and in the moonlight he looked like some Greek god come to earth. I wondered how he could stand being so handsome. Then I sighed. I didn't quite get what he meant about Darry. Darry thought I was just another mouth to feed and somebody to holler at. Darry love me? I thought of those hard, pale eyes. Soda was wrong for once, I thought. Darry doesn't love anyone or anything, except maybe Soda. I didn't hardly think of him as being human. I don't care, I lied to myself, I don't care about him either. Soda's enough, and I'd have him until I got out of school. I don't care about Darry. But I was still lying and I knew it. I lie to myself all the time. But I never believe me.

Chapter 2

DALLY WAS WAITING for Johnny and me under the street light at the corner of Pickett and Sutton, and since we got there early, we had time to go over to the drugstore in the shopping center and goof around. We bought Cokes and blew the straws at the waitress, and walked around eyeing things that were lying out in the open until the manager got wise to us and suggested we leave. He was too late, though; Dally walked out with two packages of Kools under his jacket.

Then we went across the street and down Sutton a little way to The Dingo. There are lots of drive-ins in town—the Socs go to The Way Out and to Rusty's, and the greasers go to The Dingo and to Jay's. The Dingo is a pretty rough hangout; there's always a fight going on there and once a girl got shot. We walked around talking to all the greasers and hoods we knew, leaning in car windows or hopping into the back seats, and getting in on who was running away, and who was in jail, and who was going with who, and who could whip who, and who stole what and when and why. We knew about everybody there. There was a pretty good fight while we were there between a big twenty-three-year-old greaser and a Mexican hitchhiker. We left when the switchblades came out, because the cops would be coming soon and nobody in his right mind wants to be around when the fuzz show.

We crossed Sutton and cut around behind Spencer's Special, the discount house, and chased two junior-high kids across a field for a few minutes; by then it was dark enough to sneak in over the back fence of the Nightly Double drive-in movie. It was the biggest in town, and showed two movies every night, and on weekends four—you could say you were going to the Nightly Double and have time to go all over town.

We all had the money to get in—it only costs a quarter if you're not in a car—but Dally hated to do things the legal way. He liked to show that he didn't care whether there was a law or not. He went around *trying* to break laws. We went to the rows of seats in front of the concession stand to sit down. Nobody else was there except two girls who were sitting down front. Dally eyed them coolly, then walked down the aisle and sat right behind them. I had a sick feeling that Dally was up to his usual tricks, and I was right. He started talking, loud enough for the two girls to hear. He started out bad and got worse. Dallas could talk awful dirty if he wanted to and I guess he wanted to then. I felt my ears get hot. Two-Bit or Steve or even Soda would have gone right along with him, just to see if they could embarrass the girls, but that kind of kicks just doesn't appeal to me. I sat there, struck dumb, and Johnny left hastily to get a Coke.

I wouldn't have felt so embarrassed if they had been greasy girls—I might even have helped old Dallas. But those two girls weren't our kind. They were tuff-looking girls—dressed sharp and really good-looking. They looked about sixteen or seventeen. One had short dark hair, and the other had long red hair. The redhead was getting mad, or scared. She sat up straight and she was chewing hard on her gum. The other one pretended not to hear Dally. Dally was getting impatient. He put his feet up on the back of the redhead's chair, winked at me, and beat his own record for saying something dirty. She turned around and gave him a cool stare.

"Take your feet off my chair and shut your trap."

Boy, she was good-looking. I'd seen her before; she was a cheerleader at our school. I'd always thought she was stuck-up.

Dally merely looked at her and kept his feet where they were. "Who's gonna make me?"

The other one turned around and watched us. "That's the greaser that jockeys for the Slash J sometimes," she said, as if we couldn't hear her.

I had heard the same tone a million times: "Greaser . . . greaser . . . greaser." Oh yeah, I had heard that tone before too many times. What are they doing at a drive-in without a car? I thought, and Dallas said, "I know you two. I've seen you around rodeos."

"It's a shame you can't ride bull half as good as you can

talk it," the redhead said coolly and turned back around.

That didn't bother Dally in the least. "You two barrel race, huh?"

"You'd better leave us alone," the redhead said in a biting voice, "or I'll call the cops."

"Oh, my, my"—Dally looked bored—"you've got me scared to death. You ought to see my record sometime, baby." He grinned slyly. "Guess what I've been in for?"

"*Please* leave us alone," she said. "Why don't you be nice and leave us alone?"

Dally grinned roguishly. "I'm never nice. Want a Coke?"

She was mad by then. "I wouldn't drink it if I was starving in the desert. Get lost, hood!"

Dally merely shrugged and strolled off.

The girl looked at me. I was half-scared of her. I'm half-scared of all nice girls, especially Socs. "Are *you* going to start in on us?"

I shook my head, wide-eyed. "No."

Suddenly she smiled. Gosh, she was pretty. "You don't look the type. What's your name?"

I wished she hadn't asked me that. I hate to tell people my name for the first time. "Ponyboy Curtis."

Then I waited for the "You're kidding!" or "That's your *real* name?" or one of the other remarks I usually get. Ponyboy's my real name and personally I like it.

The redhead just smiled. "That's an original and lovely name."

"My dad was an original person," I said. "I've got a brother named Sodapop, and it says so on his birth certificate."

"My name's Sherri, but I'm called Cherry because of my hair. Cherry Valance."

"I know," I said. "You're a cheerleader. We go to the same school."

"You don't look old enough to be going to high school," the dark-haired girl said.

"I'm not. I got put up a year in grade school."

Cherry was looking at me. "What's a nice, smart kid like you running around with trash like that for?"

I felt myself stiffen. "I'm a grease, same as Dally. He's my buddy."

"I'm sorry, Ponyboy," she said softly. Then she said briskly, "Your brother Sodapop, does he work at a gasoline station? A DX, I think?"

"Yeah."

"Man, your brother is one doll. I might have guessed you were brothers—you look alike."

I grinned with pride—I don't think I look one bit like Soda, but it's not every day I hear Socs telling me they think my brother is a doll.

"Didn't he used to ride in rodeos? Saddle bronc?"

"Yeah. Dad made him quit after he tore a ligament, though. We still hang around rodeos a lot. I've seen you two barrel race. You're good."

"Thanks," Cherry said, and the other girl, who was named Marcia, said, "How come we don't see your brother at school? He's not any older than sixteen or seventeen, is he?"

I winced inside. I've told you I can't stand it that Soda dropped out. "He's a dropout," I said roughly. "Dropout" made me think of some poor dumb-looking hoodlum wandering the streets breaking out street lights—it didn't fit my happy-go-lucky brother at all. It fitted Dally perfectly, but you could hardly say it about Soda.

Johnny came back then and sat down beside me. He looked around for Dally, then managed a shy "Hi" to the girls and tried to watch the movie. He was nervous, though. Johnny was always nervous around strangers. Cherry looked at him, sizing him up as she had me. Then she smiled softly, and I knew she had him sized up right.

Dally came striding back with an armful of Cokes. He handed one to each of the girls and sat down beside Cherry. "This might cool you off."

She gave him an incredulous look; and then she threw her Coke in his face. "That might cool *you* off, greaser. After you wash your mouth and learn to talk and act decent, I might cool off, too."

Dally wiped the Coke off his face with his sleeve and smiled dangerously. If I had been Cherry I would have beat it out of there. I knew that smile.

"Fiery, huh? Well, that's the way I like 'em." He started to put his arm around her, but Johnny reached over and stopped him.

"Leave her alone, Dally."

"Huh?" Dally was taken off guard. He stared at Johnny in disbelief. Johnny couldn't say "Boo" to a goose. Johnny gulped and got a little pale, but he said, "You heard me. Leave her alone."

Dallas scowled for a second. If it had been me, or Two-Bit, or Soda or Steve, or anyone but Johnny, Dally would have flattened him without a moment's hesitation. You just didn't tell Dally Winston what to do. One time, in a dime store, a guy told him to move over at the candy counter. Dally had turned around and belted him so hard it knocked a tooth loose. A complete stranger, too. But

Johnny was the gang's pet, and Dally just couldn't hit him. He was Dally's pet, too. Dally got up and stalked off, his fists jammed in his pockets and a frown on his face. He didn't come back.

Cherry sighed in relief. "Thanks. He had me scared to death."

Johnny managed an admiring grin. "You sure didn't show it. Nobody talks to Dally like that."

She smiled. "From what I saw, you do."

Johnny's ears got red. I was still staring at him. It had taken more than nerve for him to say what he'd said to Dally—Johnny worshiped the ground Dallas walked on, and I had never heard Johnny talk back to anyone, much less his hero.

Marcia grinned at us. She was a little smaller than Cherry. She was cute, but that Cherry Valance was a real looker. "Y'all sit up here with us. You can protect us."

Johnny and I looked at each other. He grinned suddenly, raising his eyebrows so that they disappeared under his bangs. Would we ever have something to tell the boys! his eyes said plainly. We had picked up two girls, and classy ones at that. Not any greasy broads for us, but real Socs. Soda would flip when I told him.

"Okay," I said nonchalantly, "might as well."

I sat between them, and Johnny sat next to Cherry.

"How old are y'all?" Marcia asked.

"Fourteen," I said.

"Sixteen," said Johnny.

"That's funny," Marcia said, "I thought you were both . . ."

"Sixteen," Cherry finished for her.

I was grateful. Johnny looked fourteen and he knew

it and it bugged him something awful.

Johnny grinned. "How come y'all ain't scared of us like you were Dally?"

Cherry sighed. "You two are too sweet to scare anyone. First of all, you didn't join in Dallas's dirty talk, and you made him leave us alone. And when we asked you to sit up here with us, you didn't act like it was an invitation to make out for the night. Besides that, I've heard about Dallas Winston, and he looked as hard as nails and twice as tough. And you two don't look mean."

"Sure," I said tiredly, "we're young and innocent."

"No," Cherry said slowly, looking at me carefully, "not innocent. You've seen too much to be innocent. Just not . . . dirty."

"Dally's okay," Johnny said defensively, and I nodded. You take up for your buddies, no matter what they do. When you're a gang, you stick up for the members. If you don't stick up for them, stick together, make like brothers, it isn't a gang any more. It's a pack. A snarling, distrustful, bickering pack like the Socs in their social clubs or the street gangs in New York or the wolves in the timber. "He's tough, but he's a cool old guy."

"He'd leave you alone if he knew you," I said, and that was true. When Steve's cousin from Kansas came down, Dally was decent to her and watched his swearing. We all did around nice girls who were the cousinly type. I don't know how to explain it—we try to be nice to the girls we see once in a while, like cousins or the girls in class; but we still watch a nice girl go by on a street corner and say all kinds of lousy stuff about her. Don't ask me why. I don't know why.

"Well," Marcia said with finality, "I'm glad he doesn't know us."

"I kind of admire him," Cherry said softly, so only I heard, and then we settled down to watch the movie.

Oh, yeah, we found out why they were without a car. They'd come with their boyfriends, but walked out on them when they found out the boys had brought some booze along. The boys had gotten angry and left.

"I don't care if they did." Cherry sounded annoyed. "It's not my idea of a good time to sit in a drive-in and watch people get drunk."

You could tell by the way she said it that her idea of a good time was probably high-class, and probably expensive. They'd decided to stay and see the movie anyway. It was one of those beach-party movies with no plot and no acting but a lot of girls in bikinis and some swinging songs, so it was all right. We were all four sitting there in silence when suddenly a strong hand came down on Johnny's shoulder and another on mine and a deep voice said, "Okay, greasers, you've had it."

I almost jumped out of my skin. It was like having someone leap out from behind a door and yell "Boo!" at you.

I looked fearfully over my shoulder and there was Two-Bit, grinning like a Chessy cat. "Glory, Two-Bit, scare us to death!" He was good at voice imitations and had sounded for all the world like a snarling Soc. Then I looked at Johnny. His eyes were shut and he was as white as a ghost. His breath was coming in smothered gasps. Two-Bit knew better than to scare Johnny like that. I guess he'd forgotten. He's kind of scatterbrained. Johnny opened his eyes and said weakly, "Hey, Two-Bit."

Two-Bit messed up his hair, "Sorry, kid," he said, "I forgot."

He climbed over the chair and plopped down beside Marcia. "Who's this, your great-aunts?"

"Great-grandmothers, twice removed," Cherry said smoothly.

I couldn't tell if Two-Bit was drunk or not. It's kind of hard to tell with him—he acts boozed up sometimes even when he's sober. He cocked one eyebrow up and the other down, which he always does when something puzzles him, or bothers him, or when he feels like saying something smart. "Shoot, you're ninety-six if you're a day."

"I'm a night," Marcia said brightly.

Two-Bit stared at her admiringly. "Brother, you're a sharp one. Where'd you two ever get to be picked up by a couple of greasy hoods like Pony and Johnny?"

"We really picked them up," Marcia said. "We're really Arabian slave traders and we're thinking about shanghaiing them. They're worth ten camels apiece at least."

"Five," Two-Bit disagreed. "They don't talk Arabian, I don't think. Say somethin' in Arabian, Johnnycake."

"Aw, cut it out!" Johnny broke in. "Dally was bothering them and when he left they wanted us to sit with them to protect them. Against wisecracking greasers like you, probably."

Two-Bit grinned, because Johnny didn't usually get sassy like that. We thought we were doing good if we could get him to talk at all. Incidentally, we don't mind being called greaser by another greaser. It's kind of playful then.

"Hey, where is ol' Dally, anyways?"

"He went hunting some action—booze or dames or a fight. I hope he don't get jailed again. He just got out."

"He'll probably find the fight," Two-Bit stated cheerfully. "That's why I came over. Mr. Timothy Shepard and Co. are looking for whoever so kindly slashed their car's tires, and since Mr. Curly Shepard spotted Dallas doing it . . . well . . . Does Dally have a blade?"

"Not that I know of," I said. "I think he's got a piece of pipe, but he busted his blade this morning."

"Good.(Tim'll fight fair if Dally don't pull a blade on him.)Dally shouldn't have any trouble."

Cherry and Marcia were staring at us. "You don't believe in playing rough or anything, do you?"

"A fair fight isn't rough," Two-Bit said. "Blades are rough. So are chains and heaters and pool sticks and rumbles. Skin fighting isn't rough. It blows off steam better than anything. There's nothing wrong with throwing a few punches. Socs are rough. They gang up on one or two, or they rumble each other with their social clubs. Us greasers usually stick together, but when we do fight among ourselves, it's a fair fight between two. And Dally deserves whatever he gets, 'cause slashed tires ain't no joke when you've got to work to pay for them. He got spotted, too, and that was his fault. Our one rule, besides Stick together, is Don't get caught. He might get beat up, he might not. Either way there's not going to be any blood feud between our outfit and Shepard's. If we needed them tomorrow they'd show. If Tim beats Dally's head in, and then tomorrow asks us for help in a rumble, we'll show. Dally was getting kicks. He got caught. He pays up. No sweat."

"Yeah, boy," Cherry said sarcastically, "real simple."

"Sure," Marcia said, unconcerned. "If he gets killed or something, you just bury him. No sweat."

"You dig okay, baby." Two-Bit grinned and lit a cigarette. "Anyone want a weed?"

I looked at Two-Bit admiringly. He sure put things into words good. Maybe he was still a junior at eighteen and a half, and maybe his sideburns were too long, and maybe he did get boozed up too much, but he sure understood things.

Cherry and Marcia shook their heads at his offering of cigarettes, but Johnny and I reached for one. Johnny's color was back and his breathing was regular, but his hand was shaking ever so slightly. A cigarette would steady it.

"Ponyboy, will you come with me to get some popcorn?" Cherry asked.

I jumped up. "Sure. Y'all want some?"

"I do," said Marcia. She was finishing the Coke Dally had given her. I realized then that Marcia and Cherry weren't alike. Cherry had said she wouldn't drink Dally's Coke if she was starving, and she meant it. It was the principle of the thing. But Marcia saw no reason to throw away a perfectly good, free Coke.

"Me too," said Two-Bit. He flipped me a fifty-cent piece. "Get Johnny some, too. I'm buyin'," he added as Johnny started to reach into his jeans pocket.

We went to the concession stand and, as usual, there was a line a mile long, so we had to wait. Quite a few kids turned to look at us—you didn't see a kid grease and a Socy cheerleader together often. Cherry didn't seem to notice.

"Your friend—the one with the sideburns—he's okay?"

"He ain't dangerous like Dallas if that's what you mean. He's okay."

She smiled and her eyes showed that her mind was on something else. "Johnny . . . he's been hurt bad sometime, hasn't he?" It was more of a statement than a question. "Hurt and scared."

"It was the Socs," I said nervously, because there were plenty of Socs milling around and some of them were giving me funny looks, as if I shouldn't be with Cherry or something. And I don't like to talk about it either—Johnny getting beat up, I mean. But I started in, talking a little faster than I usually do because I don't like to think about it either.

It was almost four months ago. I had walked down to the DX station to get a bottle of pop and to see Steve and Soda, because they'll always buy me a couple of bottles and let me help work on the cars. I don't like to go on weekends because then there is usually a bunch of girls down there flirting with Soda—all kinds of girls, Socs too. I don't care too much for girls yet. Soda says I'll grow out of it. He did.

It was a warmish spring day with the sun shining bright, but it was getting chilly and dark by the time we started for home. We were walking because we had left Steve's car at the station. At the corner of our block there's a wide, open field where we play football and hang out, and it's often a site for rumbles and fist fights. We were passing it, kicking rocks down the street and finishing our last bottle of Pepsi, when Steve noticed something lying on the ground. He picked it up. It was Johnny's blue-jeans jacket—the only jacket he had.

"Looks like Johnny forgot his jacket," Steve said, slinging it over his shoulder to take it by Johnny's house. Suddenly he stopped and examined it more carefully. There was a stain the color of rust across the collar. He looked at the ground. There were some more stains on the grass. He looked up and across the field with a stricken expression on his face. I think we all heard the low moan and saw the dark motionless hump on the other side of the lot at the same time. Soda reached him first. Johnny was lying face down on the ground. Soda turned him over gently, and I nearly got sick. Someone had beaten him badly.

We were used to seeing Johnny banged up—his father clobbered him around a lot, and although it made us madder than heck, we couldn't do anything about it. But those beatings had been nothing like this. Johnny's face was cut up and bruised and swollen, and there was a wide gash from his temple to his cheekbone. He would carry that scar all his life. His white T-shirt was splattered with blood. I just stood there, trembling with sudden cold. I thought he might be dead; surely nobody could be beaten like that and live. Steve closed his eyes for a second and muffled a groan as he dropped on his knees beside Soda.

Somehow the gang sensed what had happened. Two-Bit was suddenly there beside me, and for once his comical grin was gone and his dancing gray eyes were stormy. Darry had seen us from our porch and ran toward us, suddenly skidding to a halt. Dally was there, too, swearing under his breath, and turning away with a sick expression on his face. I wondered about it vaguely. Dally had seen people killed on the streets of New York's West Side. Why did he look sick now?

"Johnny?" Soda lifted him up and held him against his shoulder. He gave the limp body a slight shake. "Hey, Johnnycake."

Johnny didn't open his eyes, but there came a soft question. "Soda?"

"Yeah, it's me," Sodapop said. "Don't talk. You're gonna be okay."

"There was a whole bunch of them," Johnny went on, swallowing, ignoring Soda's command. "A blue Mustang full . . . I got so scared . . ." He tried to swear, but suddenly started crying, fighting to control himself, then sobbing all the more because he couldn't. I had seen Johnny take a whipping with a two-by-four from his old man and never let out a whimper. That made it worse to see him break now. Soda just held him and pushed Johnny's hair back out of his eyes. "It's okay, Johnnycake, they're gone now. It's okay."

Finally, between sobs, Johnny managed to gasp out his story. He had been hunting our football to practice a few kicks when a blue Mustang had pulled up beside the lot. There were four Socs in it. They had caught him and one of them had a lot of rings on his hand—that's what had cut Johnny up so badly. It wasn't just that they had beaten him half to death—he could take that. They had scared him. They had threatened him with everything under the sun. Johnny was high-strung anyway, a nervous wreck from getting belted every time he turned around and from hearing his parents fight all the time. Living in those conditions might have turned someone else rebellious and bitter; it was killing Johnny. He had never been a coward. He was a good man in a rumble. He stuck up for the gang and kept his mouth shut good around cops. But after the night of the beating, Johnny was jumpier than ever. I didn't think he'd ever get over it. Johnny never walked by himself after that. And Johnny, who was the most law-abiding of us, now carried in his back pocket a six-inch switchblade. He'd use it, too, if he ever got jumped again. They had scared him that much. He would kill the next person who jumped him. Nobody was ever going to beat him like that again. Not over his dead body . . .

I had nearly forgotten that Cherry was listening to me. But when I came back to reality and looked at her, I was startled to find her as white as a sheet.

"All Socs aren't like that," she said. "You have to believe me, Ponyboy. Not all of us are like that."

"Sure," I said.

"That's like saying all you greasers are like Dallas Winston. I'll bet he's jumped a few people."

I digested that. It was true. Dally had jumped people. He had told us stories about muggings in New York that made the hair on the back of my neck stand up. But not all of us were that bad.

Cherry no longer looked sick, only sad. "I'll bet you think the Socs have it made. The rich kids, the West-side Socs. I'll tell you something, Ponyboy, and it may come as a surprise. We have troubles you've never even heard of. You want to know something?" She looked me straight in the eye. "Things are rough all over."

"I believe you," I said. "We'd better get back out there with the popcorn or Two-Bit'll think I ran off with his money."

We went back and watched the movie through again. Marcia and Two-Bit were hitting it off fine. Both had the same scatterbrained sense of humor. But Cherry and Johnny and I just sat there, looking at the movie and not talking. I quit worrying about everything and thought about how nice it was to sit with a girl without having to listen to her swear or to beat her off with a club. I knew Johnny liked it, too. He didn't talk to girls much. Once, while Dallas was in reform school, Sylvia had started hanging on to Johnny and sweet-talking him and Steve got hold of her and told her if she tried any of her tricks with Johnny he'd personally beat the tar out of her. Then he gave Johnny a lecture on girls and how a sneaking little broad like Sylvia would get him into a lot of trouble. As a result, Johnny never spoke to girls much, but whether that was because he was scared of Steve or because he was shy, I couldn't tell.

I got the same lecture from Two-Bit after we'd picked up a couple of girls downtown one day. I thought it was funny, because girls are one subject even Darry thinks I use my head about. And it really had been funny, because Two-Bit was half-crocked when he gave me the lecture, and he told me some stories that about made me want to crawl under the floor or something. But he had been talking about girls like Sylvia and the girls he and Dally and the rest picked up at drive-ins and downtown; he never said anything about Socy girls. So I figured it was all right to be sitting there with them. Even if they did have their own troubles. I really couldn't see what Socs would have to sweat about—good grades, good cars, good girls, madras and Mustangs and Corvairs—Man, I thought, if I had worries like that I'd consider myself lucky.

I know better now.

Chapter 3

AFTER THE MOVIE was over it suddenly came to us that Cherry and Marcia didn't have a way to get home. Two-Bit gallantly offered to walk them home—the west side of town was only about twenty miles away—but they wanted to call their parents and have them come and get them. Two-Bit finally talked them into letting us drive them home in his car. I think they were still half-scared of us. They were getting over it, though, as we walked to Two-Bit's house to pick up the car. It seemed funny to me that Socs—if these girls were any example—were just like us. They liked the Beatles and thought Elvis Presley was out, and we thought the Beatles were rank and that Elvis was tuff, but that seemed the only difference to me. Of course greasy girls would have acted a lot tougher, but there was a basic sameness. I thought maybe it was money that separated us.

"No," Cherry said slowly when I said this. "It's not just money. Part of it is, but not all. You greasers have a different set of values. You're more emotional. We're sophisticated—cool to the point of not feeling anything. Nothing is real with us. You know, sometimes I'll catch myself talking to a girl-friend, and realize I don't mean half of what I'm saying. I don't really think a beer blast on the river bottom is super-cool, but I'll rave about one to a girl-friend just to be saying something." She smiled at me. "I never told anyone that. I think you're the first person I've ever really gotten through to."

She was coming through to me all right, probably because I was a greaser, and younger; she didn't have to keep her guard up with me.

"Rat race is a perfect name for it," she said. "We're always going and going and going, and never asking where. Did you ever hear of having more than you wanted? So that you couldn't want anything else and then started looking for something else to want? It seems like we're always searching for something to satisfy us, and never finding it. Maybe if we could lose our cool we could."

That was the truth. Socs were always behind a wall of aloofness, careful not to let their real selves show through. I had seen a social-club rumble once. The Socs even fought coldly and practically and impersonally.

"That's why we're separated," I said. "It's not money, it's feeling—you don't feel anything and we feel too violently."

"And"—she was trying to hide a smile—"that's probably why we take turns getting our names in the paper."

Two-Bit and Marcia weren't even listening to us. They

were engaged in some wild conversation that made no sense to anyone but themselves.

I have quite a rep for being quiet, almost as quiet as Johnny. Two-Bit always said he wondered why Johnny and I were such good buddies. "You must make such interestin' conversation," he'd say, cocking one eyebrow, "you keepin' your mouth shut and Johnny not sayin' anything." But Johnny and I understood each other without saying anything. Nobody but Soda could really get me talking. Till I met Cherry Valance.

I don't know why I could talk to her; maybe for the same reason she could talk to me. The first thing I knew I was telling her about Mickey Mouse, Soda's horse. I had never told anyone about Soda's horse. It was personal.

Soda had this buckskin horse, only it wasn't his. It belonged to a guy who kept it at the stables where Soda used to work. Mickey Mouse was Soda's horse, though. The first day Soda saw him he said, "There's my horse," and I never doubted it. I was about ten then. Sodapop is horsecrazy. I mean it. He's always hanging around stables and rodeos, hopping on a horse every time he gets a chance. When I was ten I thought that Mickey Mouse and Soda looked alike and were alike. Mickey Mouse was a dark-gold buckskin, sassy and ornery, not much more than a colt. He'd come when Soda called him. He wouldn't come for anyone else. That horse loved Soda. He'd stand there and chew on Soda's sleeve or collar. Gosh, but Sodapop was crazy about that horse. He went down to see him every day. Mickey Mouse was a mean horse. He kicked other horses and was always getting into trouble. "I've got me a ornery pony," Soda'd tell him, rubbing his

neck. "How come you're so mean, Mickey Mouse?"
Mickey Mouse would just chew on his sleeve and sometimes nip him. But not hard. He may have belonged to
another guy, but he was Soda's horse.

"Does Soda still have him?" Cherry asked.

"He got sold," I said. "They came and got him one day
and took him off. He was a real valuable horse. Pure
quarter."

She didn't say anything else and I was glad. I couldn't
tell her that Soda had bawled all night long after they
came and got Mickey Mouse. I had cried, too, if you want
to know the truth, because Soda never really wanted anything except a horse, and he'd lost his. Soda had been
twelve then, going-on-thirteen. He never let on to Mom
and Dad how he felt, though, because we never had
enough money and usually we had a hard time making
ends meet. When you're thirteen in our neighborhood you
know the score. I kept saving my money for a year, thinking that someday I could buy Mickey Mouse back for
Soda. You're not so smart at ten.

"You read a lot, don't you, Ponyboy?" Cherry asked.

I was startled. "Yeah. Why?"

She kind of shrugged. "I could just tell. I'll bet you
watch sunsets, too." She was quiet for a minute after I nodded. "I used to watch them, too, before I got so busy . . ."

I pictured that, or tried to. Maybe Cherry stood still and
watched the sun set while she was supposed to be taking
the garbage out. Stood there and watched and forgot everything else until her big brother screamed at her to hurry
up. I shook my head. It seemed funny to me that the sunset she saw from her patio and the one I saw from the back

steps was the same one. Maybe the two different worlds we lived in weren't so different. We saw the same sunset.

Marcia suddenly gasped. "Cherry, look what's coming."

We all looked and saw a blue Mustang coming down the street. Johnny made a small noise in his throat and when I looked at him he was white.

Marcia was shifting nervously. "What are we going to do?"

Cherry bit a fingernail. "Stand here," she said. "There isn't much else we can do."

"Who is it?" Two-Bit asked. "The F.B.I.?"

"No," Cherry said bleakly, "it's Randy and Bob."

"And," Two-Bit added grimly, "a few other of the socially elite checkered-shirt set."

"Your boyfriends?" Johnny's voice was steady, but standing as close to him as I was, I could see he was trembling. I wondered why—Johnny was a nervous wreck, but he never was that jumpy.

Cherry started walking down the street. "Maybe they won't see us. Act normal."

"Who's acting?" Two-Bit grinned. "I'm a natural normal."

"Wish it was the other way around," I muttered, and Two-Bit said, "Don't get mouthy, Ponyboy."

The Mustang passed us slowly and went right on by. Marcia sighed in relief. "That was close."

Cherry turned to me. "Tell me about your oldest brother. You don't talk much about him."

I tried to think of something to say about Darry, and shrugged. "What's to talk about? He's big and handsome and likes to play football."

"I mean, what's he like? I feel like I know Soda from the

way you talk about him; tell me about Darry." And when I
was silent she urged me on. "Is he wild and reckless like
Soda? Dreamy, like you?"

My face got hot as I bit my lip. Darry . . . what was
Darry like? "He's . . ." I started to say he was a good ol' guy
but I couldn't. I burst out bitterly: "He's not like Sodapop
at all and he sure ain't like me. He's hard as a rock and
about as human. He's got eyes exactly like frozen ice. He
thinks I'm a pain in the neck. He likes Soda—everybody
likes Soda—but he can't stand me. I bet he wishes he
could stick me in a home somewhere, and he'd do it, too,
if Soda'd let him."

Two-Bit and Johnny were staring at me now. "No . . ."
Two-Bit said, dumfounded. "No, Ponyboy, that ain't right
. . . you got it wrong . . ."

"Gee," Johnny said softly, "I thought you and Darry and
Soda got along real well . . ."

"Well, we don't," I snapped, feeling silly. I knew my ears
were red by the way they were burning, and I was thankful
for the darkness. I felt stupid. Compared to Johnny's
home, mine was heaven. At least Darry didn't get drunk
and beat me up or run me out of the house, and I had
Sodapop to talk things over with. That made me mad, I
mean making a fool of myself in front of everyone. "An'
you can shut your trap, Johnny Cade, 'cause we all know
you ain't wanted at home, either. And you can't blame
them."

Johnny's eyes went round and he winced as though I'd
belted him. Two-Bit slapped me a good one across the side
of the head, and hard.

"Shut your mouth, kid. If you wasn't Soda's kid brother

I'd beat the tar out of you. You know better than to talk to Johnny like that." He put his hand on Johnny's shoulder. "He didn't mean it, Johnny."

"I'm sorry," I said miserably. Johnny was my buddy. "I was just mad."

"It's the truth," Johnny said with a bleak grin. "I don't care."

"Shut up talkin' like that," Two-Bit said fiercely, messing up Johnny's hair. "We couldn't get along without you, so you can just shut up!"

"It ain't fair!" I cried passionately. "It ain't fair that we have all the rough breaks!" I didn't know exactly what I meant, but I was thinking about Johnny's father being a drunk and his mother a selfish slob, and Two-Bit's mother being a barmaid to support him and his kid sister after their father ran out on them, and Dally—wild, cunning Dally—turning into a hoodlum because he'd die if he didn't, and Steve—his hatred for his father coming out in his soft, bitter voice and the violence of his temper. Sodapop . . . a dropout so he could get a job and keep me in school, and Darry, getting old before his time trying to run a family and hold on to two jobs and never having any fun—while the Socs had so much spare time and money that they jumped us and each other for kicks, had beer blasts and river-bottom parties because they didn't know what else to do. Things were rough all over, all right. All over the East Side. It just didn't seem right to me.

"I know," Two-Bit said with a good-natured grin, "the chips are always down when it's our turn, but that's the way things are. Like it or lump it."

Cherry and Marcia didn't say anything. I guess they

didn't know what to say. We had forgotten they were there. Then the blue Mustang was coming down the street again, more slowly.

"Well," Cherry said resignedly, "they've spotted us."

The Mustang came to a halt beside us, and the two boys in the front seat got out. They were Socs all right. One had on a white shirt and a madras ski jacket, and the other a light-yellow shirt and a wine-colored sweater. I looked at their clothes and realized for the first time that evening that all I had was a pair of jeans and Soda's old navy sweat shirt with the sleeves cut short. I swallowed. Two-Bit started to tuck in his shirttail, but stopped himself in time; he just flipped up the collar of his black leather jacket and lit a cigarette. The Socs didn't even seem to see us.

"Cherry, Marcia, listen to us . . ." the handsome black-haired Soc with the dark sweater began.

Johnny was breathing heavily and I noticed he was staring at the Soc's hand. He was wearing three heavy rings. I looked quickly at Johnny, an idea dawning on me. I remembered that it was a blue Mustang that had pulled up beside the vacant lot and that Johnny's face had been cut up by someone wearing rings . . .

The Soc's voice broke into my thoughts: ". . . just because we got a little drunk last time . . ."

Cherry looked mad. "A little? You call reeling and passing out in the streets 'a little'? Bob, I told you, I'm never going out with you while you're drinking, and I mean it. Too many things could happen while you're drunk. It's me or the booze."

The other Soc, a tall guy with a semi-Beatle haircut, turned to Marcia. "Baby, you know we don't get drunk very often . . ." When she only gave him a cold stare he got angry. "And even if you are mad at us, that's no reason to go walking the streets with these bums."

Two-Bit took a long drag on his cigarette, Johnny slouched and hooked his thumbs in his pockets, and I stiffened. We can look meaner than anything when we want to—looking tough comes in handy. Two-Bit put his elbow on Johnny's shoulder. "Who you callin' bums?"

"Listen, greasers, we got four more of us in the back seat . . ."

"Then pity the back seat," Two-Bit said to the sky.

"If you're looking for a fight . . ."

Two-Bit cocked an eyebrow, but it only made him look more cool. "You mean if I'm looking for a good jumping, you outnumber us, so you'll give it to us? Well . . ." He snatched up an empty bottle, busted off the end, and gave it to me, then reached in his back pocket and flipped out his switchblade. "Try it, pal."

"No!" Cherry cried. "Stop it!" She looked at Bob. "We'll ride home with you. Just wait a minute."

"Why?" Two-Bit demanded. "We ain't scared of them."

Cherry shuddered. "I can't stand fights . . . I can't stand them . . ."

I pulled her to one side. "I couldn't use this," I said, dropping the pop bottle. "I couldn't ever cut anyone. . . ." I had to tell her that, because I'd seen her eyes when Two-Bit flicked out his switch.

"I know," she said quietly, "but we'd better go with them. Ponyboy . . . I mean . . . if I see you in the hall at school or someplace and don't say hi, well, it's not personal or anything, but . . ."

"I know," I said.

"We couldn't let our parents see us with you all. You're a nice boy and everything . . ."

"It's okay," I said, wishing I was dead and buried somewhere. Or at least that I had on a decent shirt. "We aren't in the same class. Just don't forget that some of us watch the sunset too."

She looked at me quickly. "I could fall in love with Dallas Winston," she said. "I hope I never see him again, or I will."

She left me standing there with my mouth dropped open, and the blue Mustang vroomed off.

We walked on home, mostly in silence. I wanted to ask Johnny if those were the same Socs that had beaten him up, but I didn't mention it. Johnny never talked about it and we never said anything.

"Well, those were two good-lookin' girls if I ever saw any." Two-Bit yawned as we sat down on the curb at the vacant lot. He took a piece of paper out of his pocket and tore it up.

"What was that?"

"Marcia's number. Probably a phony one, too. I must have been outa my mind to ask for it. I think I'm a little soused."

So he had been drinking. Two-Bit was smart. He knew the score. "Y'all goin' home?" he asked.

"Not right now," I said. I wanted to have another smoke and to watch the stars. I had to be in by twelve, but I thought I had plenty of time.

"I don't know why I handed you that busted bottle,"

Two-Bit said, getting to his feet. "You'd never use it."

"Maybe I would have," I said. "Where you headed?"

"Gonna go play a little snooker and hunt up a poker game. Maybe get rip-roarin' drunk. I dunno. See y'all tomorrow."

Johnny and I stretched out on our backs and looked at the stars. I was freezing—it was a cold night and all I had was that sweat shirt, but I could watch stars in sub-zero weather. I saw Johnny's cigarette glowing in the dark and wondered vaguely what it was like inside a burning ember . . .

"It was because we're greasers," Johnny said, and I knew he was talking about Cherry. "We could have hurt her reputation."

"I reckon," I said, wondering if I ought to tell Johnny what she had said about Dallas.

"Man, that was a tuff car. Mustangs are tuff."

"Big-time Socs, all right," I said, a nervous bitterness growing inside me. It wasn't fair for the Socs to have every-thing. We were as good as they were; it wasn't our fault we were greasers. I couldn't just take it or leave it, like Two-Bit, or ignore it and love life anyway, like Sodapop, or harden myself beyond caring, like Dally, or actually enjoy it, like Tim Shepard. I felt the tension growing inside of me and I knew something had to happen or I would explode.

"I can't take much more." Johnny spoke my own feel-ings. "I'll kill myself or something."

"Don't," I said, sitting up in alarm. "You can't kill your-self, Johnny."

"Well, I won't. But I gotta do something. It seems like there's gotta be someplace without greasers or Socs, with just people. Plain ordinary people."

"Out of the big towns," I said, lying back down. "In the country . . ."

In the country . . . I loved the country. I wanted to be out of towns and away from excitement. I only wanted to lie on my back under a tree and read a book or draw a picture, and not worry about being jumped or carrying a blade or ending up married to some scatterbrained broad with no sense. The country would be like that, I thought dreamily. I would have a yeller cur dog, like I used to, and Sodapop could get Mickey Mouse back and ride in all the rodeos he wanted to, and Darry would lose that cold, hard look and be like he used to be, eight months ago, before Mom and Dad were killed. Since I was dreaming I brought Mom and Dad back to life . . . Mom could bake some more chocolate cakes and Dad would drive the pickup out early to feed the cattle. He would slap Darry on the back and tell him he was getting to be a man, a regular chip off the block, and they would be as close as they used to be. Maybe Johnny could come and live with us, and the gang could come out on weekends, and maybe Dallas would see that there was some good in the world after all, and Mom would talk to him and make him grin in spite of himself. "You've got quite a mom," Dally used to say. "She knows the score." She could talk to Dallas and kept him from getting into a lot of trouble. My mother was golden and beautiful . . .

"Ponyboy"—Johnny was shaking me—"Hey, Pony, wake up."

I sat up, shivering. The stars had moved. "Glory, what time is it?"

"I don't know. I went to sleep, too, listening to you rattle on and on. You'd better get home. I think I'll stay all night out here." Johnny's parents didn't care if he came home or not.

"Okay." I yawned. Gosh, but it was cold. "If you get cold or something come on over to our house."

"Okay."

I ran home, trembling at the thought of facing Darry. The porch light was on. Maybe they were asleep and I could sneak in, I thought. I peeked in the window. Sodapop was stretched out on the sofa, sound asleep, but Darry was in the armchair under the lamp, reading the newspaper. I gulped, and opened the door softly. Darry looked up from his paper. He was on his feet in a second. I stood there, chewing on my fingernail.

"Where the heck have you been? Do you know what time it is?" He was madder than I'd seen him in a long time. I shook my head wordlessly.

"Well, it's two in the morning, kiddo. Another hour and I would have had the police out after you. Where were you, Ponyboy?"—his voice was rising—"Where in the almighty universe were you?"

It sounded dumb, even to me, when I stammered, "I . . . I went to sleep in the lot . . ."

"You what?" He was shouting, and Sodapop sat up and rubbed his eyes.

"Hey, Ponyboy," he said sleepily, "where ya been?"

"I didn't mean to." I pleaded with Darry. "I was talking to Johnny and we both dropped off . . ."

"I reckon it never occurred to you that your brothers might be worrying their heads off and afraid to call the police because something like that could get you two thrown in a boys' home so quick it'd make your head spin. And you were asleep in the lot? Ponyboy, what on earth is the matter with you? Can't you use your head? You haven't even got a coat on."

I felt hot tears of anger and frustration rising. "I said I didn't mean to . . ."

"I didn't mean to!" Darry shouted, and I almost shook. "I didn't think! I forgot! That's all I hear out of you! Can't you think of anything?"

"Darry . . ." Sodapop began, but Darry turned on him. "You keep your trap shut! I'm sick and tired of hearin' you stick up for him."

He should never yell at Soda. Nobody should ever holler at my brother. I exploded. "You don't yell at him!" I shouted. Darry wheeled around and slapped me so hard that it knocked me against the door.

Suddenly it was deathly quiet. We had all frozen. Nobody in my family had ever hit me. Nobody. Soda was wide-eyed. Darry looked at the palm of his hand where it had turned red and then looked back at me. His eyes were huge. "Ponyboy . . ."

I turned and ran out the door and down the street as fast as I could. Darry screamed, "Pony, I didn't mean to!" but I was at the lot by then and pretended I couldn't hear. I was running away. It was plain to me that Darry didn't want me around. And I wouldn't stay if he did. He wasn't ever going to hit me again.

"Johnny?" I called, and started when he rolled over and

jumped up almost under my feet. "Come on, Johnny, we're running away."

Johnny asked no questions. We ran for several blocks until we were out of breath. Then we walked. I was crying by then. I finally just sat down on the curb and cried, burying my face in my arms. Johnny sat down beside me, one hand on my shoulder. "Easy, Ponyboy," he said softly, "we'll be okay."

I finally calmed down and wiped my eyes on my bare arm. My breath was coming in quivering sobs. "Gotta cigarette?"

He handed me one and struck a match.

"Johnny, I'm scared."

"Well, don't be. You're scarin' me. What happened? I never seen you bawl like that."

"I don't very often. It was Darry. He hit me. I don't know what happened, but I couldn't take him hollering at me and hitting me too. I don't know . . . sometimes we get along okay, then all of a sudden he blows up on me or else is naggin' at me all the time. He didn't use to be like that . . . we used to get along okay . . . before Mom and Dad died. Now he just can't stand me."

"I think I like it better when the old man's hittin' me." Johnny sighed. "At least then I know he knows who I am. I walk in that house, and nobody says anything. I walk out, and nobody says anything. I stay away all night, and nobody notices. At least you got Soda. I ain't got nobody."

"Shoot," I said, startled out of my misery, "you got the whole gang. Dally didn't slug you tonight 'cause you're the pet. I mean, golly, Johnny, you got the whole gang."

"It ain't the same as having your own folks care about

you," Johnny said simply. "It just ain't the same."

I was beginning to relax and wonder if running away was such a great idea. I was sleepy and freezing to death and I wanted to be home in bed, safe and warm under the covers with Soda's arm across me. I decided I would go home and just not speak to Darry. It was my house as much as Darry's, and if he wanted to pretend I wasn't alive, that was just fine with me. He couldn't stop me from living in my own house.

"Let's walk to the park and back. Then maybe I'll be cooled off enough to go home."

"Okay," Johnny said easily. "Okay."

Things gotta get better, I figured. They couldn't get worse. I was wrong.

Chapter 4

THE PARK WAS ABOUT two blocks square, with a fountain in the middle and a small swimming pool for the little kids. The pool was empty now in the fall, but the fountain was going merrily. Tall elm trees made the park shadowy and dark, and it would have been a good hangout, but we preferred our vacant lot, and the Shepard outfit liked the alleys down by the tracks, so the park was left to lovers and little kids.

Nobody was around at two-thirty in the morning, and it was a good place to relax and cool off. I couldn't have gotten much cooler without turning into a popsicle. Johnny snapped up his jeans jacket and flipped up the collar.

"Ain't you about to freeze to death, Pony?"

"You ain't a'woofin'," I said, rubbing my bare arms between drags on my cigarette. I started to say something about the film of ice developing on the outer edges of the fountain when a sudden blast from a car horn made us both jump. The blue Mustang was circling the park slowly.

Johnny swore under his breath, and I muttered, "What do they want? This is our territory. What are Socs doing this far east?"

Johnny shook his head. "I don't know. But I bet they're looking for us. We picked up their girls."

"Oh, glory," I said with a groan, "this is all I need to top off a perfect night." I took one last drag on my weed and ground the stub under my heel. "Want to run for it?"

"It's too late now," Johnny said. "Here they come."

Five Socs were coming straight at us, and from the way they were staggering I figured they were reeling pickled. That scared me. A cool deadly bluff could sometimes shake them off, but not if they outnumbered you five to two and were drunk. Johnny's hand went to his back pocket and I remembered his switchblade. I wished for that broken bottle. I'd sure show them I could use it if I had to. Johnny was scared to death. I mean it. He was as white as a ghost and his eyes were wild-looking, like the eyes of an animal in a trap. We backed against the fountain and the Socs surrounded us. They smelled so heavily of whiskey and English Leather that I almost choked. I wished desperately that Darry and Soda would come along hunting for me. The four of us could handle them easily. But no one was around, and I knew Johnny and I were going to have to fight it out alone. Johnny had a blank, tough look on his face—you'd have had to know him to see the panic in his eyes. I stared at the Socs coolly. Maybe they could scare us to death, but we'd never let them have the satisfaction of knowing it.

It was Randy and Bob and three other Socs, and they recognized us. I knew Johnny recognized them; he was watching the moonlight glint off Bob's rings with huge eyes.

"Hey, whatta ya know?" Bob said a little unsteadily, "here's the little greasers that picked up our girls. Hey, greasers."

"You're outa your territory," Johnny warned in a low voice. "You'd better watch it."

Randy swore at us and they stepped in closer. Bob was eyeing Johnny. "Nup, pal, yer the ones who'd better watch it. Next time you want a broad, pick up yer own kind— dirt."

I was getting mad. I was hating them enough to lose my head.

"You know what a greaser is?" Bob asked. "White trash with long hair."

I felt the blood draining from my face. I've been cussed out and sworn at, but nothing ever hit me like that did. Johnnycake made a kind of gasp and his eyes were smoldering.

"You know what a Soc is?" I said, my voice shaking with rage. "White trash with Mustangs and madras." And then, because I couldn't think of anything bad enough to call them, I spit at them.

Bob shook his head, smiling slowly. "You could use a bath, greaser. And a good working over. And we've got all night to do it. Give the kid a bath, David."

I ducked and tried to run for it, but the Soc caught my

arm and twisted it behind my back, and shoved my face into the fountain. I fought, but the hand at the back of my neck was strong and I had to hold my breath. I'm dying, I thought, and wondered what was happening to Johnny. I couldn't hold my breath any longer. I fought again desperately but only sucked in water. I'm drowning, I thought, they've gone too far . . . A red haze filled my mind and I slowly relaxed.

The next thing I knew I was lying on the pavement beside the fountain, coughing water and gasping. I lay there weakly, breathing in air and spitting out water. The wind blasted through my soaked sweat shirt and dripping hair. My teeth chattered unceasingly and I couldn't stop them. I finally pushed myself up and leaned back against the fountain, the water running down my face. Then I saw Johnny.

He was sitting next to me, one elbow on his knee, and staring straight ahead. He was a strange greenish-white, and his eyes were huger than I'd ever seen them.

"I killed him," he said slowly. "I killed that boy."

Bob, the handsome Soc, was lying there in the moonlight, doubled up and still. A dark pool was growing from him, spreading slowly over the blue-white cement. I looked at Johnny's hand. He was clutching his switchblade, and it was dark to the hilt. My stomach gave a violent jump and my blood turned icy.

"Johnny," I managed to say, fighting the dizziness, "I think I'm gonna be sick."

"Go ahead," he said in the same steady voice. "I won't look at you."

I turned my head and was quietly sick for a minute.

Then I leaned back and closed my eyes so I wouldn't see Bob lying there.

This can't be happening. This can't be happening. This can't be . . .

"You really killed him, huh, Johnny?"

"Yeah." His voice quavered slightly. "I had to. They were drowning you, Pony. They might have killed you. And they had a blade . . . they were gonna beat me up. . . ."

"Like . . ." — I swallowed — "like they did before?"

Johnny was quiet for a minute. "Yeah," he said, "like they did before."

Johnny told me what had happened: "They ran when I stabbed him. They all ran . . ."

A panic was rising in me as I listened to Johnny's quiet voice go on and on. "Johnny!" I nearly screamed. "What are we gonna do? They put you in the electric chair for killing people!" I was shaking. I want a cigarette. I want a cigarette. I want a cigarette. We had smoked our last pack. "I'm scared, Johnny. What are we gonna do?"

Johnny jumped up and dragged me up by my sweat shirt. He shook me. "Calm down, Ponyboy. Get ahold of yourself."

I hadn't realized I was screaming. I shook loose. "Okay," I said, "I'm okay now."

Johnny looked around, slapping his pockets nervously. "We gotta get outa here. Get somewhere. Run away. The police'll be here soon." I was trembling, and it wasn't all from cold. But Johnny, except for the fact that his hands were twitching, looked as cool as Darry ever had. "We'll need money. And maybe a gun. And a plan."

Money. Maybe a gun? A plan. Where in the world would we get these things?

"Dally," Johnny said with finality. "Dally'll get us outa here."

I heaved a sigh. Why hadn't I thought of that? But I never thought of anything. Dallas Winston could do anything.

"Where can we find him?"

"I think at Buck Merril's place. There's a party over there tonight. Dally said somethin' about it this afternoon."

Buck Merril was Dally's rodeo partner. He was the one who'd got Dally the job as a jockey for the Slash J. Buck raised a few quarter horses, and made most of his money on fixed races and a little bootlegging. I was under strict orders from both Darry and Soda not to get caught within ten miles of his place, which was dandy with me. I didn't like Buck Merril. He was a tall lanky cowboy with blond hair and buckteeth. Or he used to be bucktoothed before he had the front two knocked out in a fight. He was out of it. He dug Hank Williams—how gross can you get?

Buck answered the door when we knocked, and a roar of cheap music came with him. The clinking of glasses, loud, rough laughter and female giggles, and Hank Williams. It scraped on my raw nerves like sandpaper. A can of beer in one hand, Buck glared down at us. "Whatta ya want?"

"Dally!" Johnny gulped, looking back over his shoulder. "We gotta see Dally."

"He's busy," Buck snapped, and someone in his living room yelled "A-ha!" and then "Yee-ha," and the sound of it almost made my nerves snap.

"Tell him it's Pony and Johnny," I commanded. I knew

Buck, and the only way you could get anything from him was to bully him. I guess that's why Dallas could handle him so easily, although Buck was in his mid-twenties and Dally was seventeen. "He'll come."

Buck glared at me for a second, then stumbled off. He was pretty well crocked, which made me apprehensive. If Dally was drunk and in a dangerous mood. . . .

He appeared in a few minutes, clad only in a pair of low-cut blue jeans, scratching the hair on his chest. He was sober enough, and that surprised me. Maybe he hadn't been there long.

"Okay, kids, whatta ya need me for?"

As Johnny told him the story, I studied Dally, trying to figure out what there was about this tough-looking hood that a girl like Cherry Valance could love. Towheaded and shifty-eyed, Dally was anything but handsome. Yet in his hard face there was character, pride, and a savage defiance of the world. He could never love Cherry Valance back. It would be a miracle if Dally loved anything. The fight for self-preservation had hardened him beyond caring.

He didn't bat an eye when Johnny told him what had happened, only grinned and said "Good for you" when Johnny told how he had knifed the Soc. Finally Johnny finished. "We figured you could get us out if anyone could. I'm sorry we got you away from the party."

"Oh, shoot, kid" — Dally glanced contemptuously over his shoulder — "I was in the bedroom."

He suddenly stared at me. "Glory, but your ears can get red, Ponyboy."

I was remembering what usually went on in the bed-rooms at Buck's parties. Then Dally grinned in amused realization. "It wasn't anything like that, kid. I was asleep, or tryin' to be, with all this racket. Hank Williams"—he rolled his eyes and added a few adjectives after 'Hank Williams.' "Me and Shepard had a run-in and I cracked some ribs. I just needed a place to lay over." He rubbed his side ruefully. "Ol' Tim sure can pack a punch. He won't be able to see outa one eye for a week." He looked us over and sighed. "Well, wait a sec and I'll see what I can do about this mess." Then he took a good look at me. "Ponyboy, are you wet?"

"Y-y-yes-s," I stammered through chattering teeth.

"Glory hallelujah!" He opened the screen door and pulled me in, motioning for Johnny to follow. "You'll die of pneumonia 'fore the cops ever get you."

He half-dragged me into an empty bedroom, swearing at me all the way. "Get that sweat shirt off." He threw a towel at me. "Dry off and wait here. At least Johnny's got his jeans jacket. You ought to know better than to run away in just a sweat shirt, and a wet one at that. Don't you ever use your head?" He sounded so much like Darry that I stared at him. He didn't notice, and left us sitting on the bed.

Johnny lay back on it. "Wish I had me a weed."

My knees were shaking as I finished drying off, sitting there in my jeans.

Dally appeared after a minute. He carefully shut the door. "Here"—he handed us a gun and a roll of bills— "the gun's loaded. For Pete's sake, Johnny, don't point the thing at me. Here's fifty bucks. That's all I could get out of Merril tonight. He's blowin' his loot from that last race."

You might have thought it was Dally who fixed those races for Buck, being a jockey and all, but it wasn't. The last guy to suggest it lost three teeth. It's the truth. Dally rode the ponies honestly and did his best to win. It was the only thing Dally did honestly.

"Pony, do Darry and Sodapop know about this?"

I shook my head. Dally sighed. "Boy howdy, I ain't itchin' to be the one to tell Darry and get my head busted."

"Then don't tell him," I said. I hated to worry Sodapop, and would have liked to let him know I had gotten this far okay, but I didn't care if Darry worried himself gray-headed. I was too tired to tell myself I was being mean and unreasonable. I convinced myself it wouldn't be fair to make Dally tell him. Darry would beat him to death for giving us the money and the gun and getting us out of town.

"Here!" Dally handed me a shirt about sixty-million sizes too big. "It's Buck's—you an' him ain't exactly the same size, but it's dry." He handed me his worn brown leather jacket with the yellow sheep's-wool lining. "It'll get cold where you're going, but you can't risk being loaded down with blankets."

I started buttoning up the shirt. It about swallowed me. "Hop the three-fifteen freight to Windrixville," Dally instructed. "There's an old abandoned church on top of Jay Mountain. There's a pump in back so don't worry about water. Buy a week's supply of food as soon as you get there—this morning, before the story gets out, and then don't so much as stick your noses out the door. I'll be up there as soon as I think it's clear. Man, I thought New York was the only place I could get mixed up in a murder rap."

At the word "murder," Johnny made a small noise in his throat and shuddered.

Dally walked us back to the door, turning off the porch light before we stepped out. "Git goin'!" He messed up Johnny's hair. "Take care, kid," he said softly.

"Sure, Dally, thanks." And we ran into the darkness.

We crouched in the weeds beside the railroad tracks, listening to the whistle grow louder. The train slowed to a screaming halt. "Now," whispered Johnny. We ran and pulled ourselves into an open boxcar. We pressed against the side, trying to hold our breath while we listened to the railroad workers walk up and down outside. One poked his head inside, and we froze. But he didn't see us, and the boxcar rattled as the train started up.

"The first stop'll be Windrixville," Johnny said, laying the gun down gingerly. He shook his head. "I don't see why he gave me this. I couldn't shoot anybody."

Then for the first time, really, I realized what we were in for. Johnny had killed someone. Quiet, soft-spoken little Johnny, who wouldn't hurt a living thing on purpose, had taken a human life. We were really running away, with the police after us for murder and a loaded gun by our side. I wished we'd asked Dally for a pack of cigarettes. . . .

I stretched out and used Johnny's legs for a pillow. Curling up, I was thankful for Dally's jacket. It was too big, but it was warm. Not even the rattling of the train could keep me awake, and I went to sleep in a hoodlum's jacket, with a gun lying next to my hand.

I was hardly awake when Johnny and I leaped off the train into a meadow. Not until I landed in the dew and got a wet shock did I realize what I was doing. Johnny must have woke me up and told me to jump, but I didn't remember it. We lay in the tall weeds and damp grass, breathing heavily. The dawn was coming. It was lightening the sky in the east and a ray of gold touched the hills. The clouds were pink and meadow larks were singing. This is the country, I thought, half asleep. My dream's come true and I'm in the country.

"Blast it, Ponyboy"—Johnny was rubbing his legs— "you must have put my legs to sleep. I can't even stand up. I barely got off that train."

"I'm sorry. Why didn't you wake me up?"

"That's okay. I didn't want to wake you up until I had to."

"Now how do we find Jay Mountain?" I asked Johnny. I was still groggy with sleep and wanted to sleep forever right there in the dew and the dawn.

"Go ask someone. The story won't be in the paper yet. Make like a farm boy taking a walk or something."

"I don't look like a farm boy," I said. I suddenly thought of my long hair, combed back, and the slouching stride I used from habit. I looked at Johnny. He didn't look like any farm boy to me. He still reminded me of a lost puppy who had been kicked too often, but for the first time I saw him as a stranger might see him. He looked hard and tough, because of his black T-shirt and his blue jeans and jacket, and because his hair was heavily greased and so long. I saw how his hair curled behind his ears and I thought: We both need a haircut and some decent clothes.

I looked down at my worn, faded blue jeans, my too-big shirt, and Dally's worn-out jacket. They'll know we're hoods the minute they see us, I thought.

"I'll have to stay here," Johnny said, rubbing his legs. "You go down the road and ask the first person you see where Jay Mountain is." He winced at the pain in his legs. "Then come back. And for Pete's sake, run a comb through your hair and quit slouching down like a thug."

So Johnny had noticed it too. I pulled a comb from my back pocket and combed my hair carefully. "I guess I look okay now, huh, Johnny?"

He was studying me. "You know, you look an awful lot like Sodapop, the way you've got your hair and everything. I mean, except your eyes are green."

"They ain't green, they're gray," I said, reddening. "And I look about as much like Soda as you do." I got to my feet. "He's good-looking."

"Shoot," Johnny said with a grin, "you are, too."

I climbed over the barbed-wire fence without saying anything else. I could hear Johnny laughing at me, but I didn't care. I went strolling down the red dirt road, hoping my natural color would come back before I met anyone. I wonder what Darry and Sodapop are doing now, I thought, yawning. Soda had the whole bed to himself for once. I bet Darry's sorry he ever hit me. He'll really get worried when he finds out Johnny and I killed that Soc. Then, for a moment, I pictured Sodapop's face when he heard about it. I wish I was home, I thought absently, I wish I was home and still in bed. Maybe I am. Maybe I'm just dreaming . . .

It was only last night that Dally and I had sat down behind those girls at the Nightly Double. Glory, I thought with a bewildering feeling of being rushed, things are happening too quick. Too fast. I figured I couldn't get into any worse trouble than murder. Johnny and I would be hiding for the rest of our lives. Nobody but Dally would know where we were, and he couldn't tell anyone because he'd get jailed again for giving us that gun. If Johnny got caught, they'd give him the electric chair, and if they caught me, I'd be sent to a reformatory. I'd heard about reformatories from Curly Shepard and I didn't want to go to one at all. So we'd have to be hermits for the rest of our lives, and never see anyone but Dally. Maybe I'd never see Darry or Sodapop again. Or even Two-Bit or Steve. I was in the country, but I knew I wasn't going to like it as much as I'd thought I would. There are things worse than being a greaser.

I met a sunburned farmer driving a tractor down the road. I waved at him and he stopped.

"Could you tell me where Jay Mountain is?" I asked as politely as I could.

He pointed on down the road. "Follow this road to that big hill over there. That's it. Taking a walk?"

"Yessir." I managed to look sheepish. "We're playing army and I'm supposed to report to headquarters there."

I can lie so easily that it spooks me sometimes—Soda says it comes from reading so much. But then, Two-Bit lies all the time too, and he never opens a book.

"Boys will be boys," the farmer said with a grin, and I thought dully that he sounded as corn-poney as Hank

Williams. He went on and I walked back to where Johnny
was waiting.

We climbed up the road to the church, although it was a
lot farther away than it looked. The road got steeper with
every step. I was feeling kind of drunk—I always do when I
get too sleepy—and my legs got heavier and heavier. I
guess Johnny was sleepier than I was—he had stayed
awake on the train to make sure we got off at the right
place. It took us about forty-five minutes to get there. We
climbed in a back window. It was a small church, real old
and spooky and spiderwebby. It gave me the creeps.

I'd been in church before. I used to go all the time,
even after Mom and Dad were gone. Then one Sunday I
talked Soda into coming with Johnny and me. He didn't
want to come unless Steve did, and Two-Bit decided he
might as well come too. Dally was sleeping off a hangover,
and Darry was working. When Johnny and I went, we sat
in the back, trying to get something out of the sermon and
avoiding the people, because we weren't dressed so sharp
most of the time. Nobody seemed to mind, and Johnny
and I really liked to go. But that day . . . well, Soda can't sit
still long enough to enjoy a movie, much less a sermon. It
wasn't long before he and Steve and Two-Bit were throwing paper wads at each other and clowning around, and
finally Steve dropped a hymn book with a bang—accidentally, of course. Everyone in the place turned around to
look at us, and Johnny and I nearly crawled under the
pews. And then Two-Bit *waved* at them.

I hadn't been to church since.

But this church gave me a kind of creepy feeling. What do you call it? Premonition? I flopped down on the floor — and immediately decided not to do any more flopping. That floor was stone, and hard. Johnny stretched out beside me, resting his head on his arm. I started to say something to him, but I went to sleep before I could get the words out of my mouth. But Johnny didn't notice. He was asleep, too.

Chapter 5

I WOKE UP LATE IN
the afternoon. For a second I didn't know where I was. You
know how it is, when you wake up in a strange place and
wonder where in the world you are, until memory comes
rushing over you like a wave. I half convinced myself that
I had dreamed everything that had happened the night
before. I'm really home in bed, I thought. It's late and both
Darry and Sodapop are up. Darry's cooking breakfast, and
in a minute he and Soda will come in and drag me out of
bed and wrestle me down and tickle me until I think I'll
die if they don't stop. It's me and Soda's turn to do the
dishes after we eat, and then we'll all go outside and play
football. Johnny and Two-Bit and I will get Darry on our
side, since Johnny and I are so small and Darry's the best
player. It'll go like the usual weekend morning. I tried

telling myself that while I lay on the cold rock floor, wrapped up in Dally's jacket and listening to the wind rushing through the trees' dry leaves outside.

Finally I quit pretending and pushed myself up. I was stiff and sore from sleeping on that hard floor, but I had never slept so soundly. I was still groggy. I pushed off Johnny's jeans jacket, which had somehow got thrown across me, and blinked, scratching my head. It was awful quiet, with just the sound of rushing wind in the trees. Suddenly I realized that Johnny wasn't there.

"Johnny?" I called loudly, and that old wooden church echoed me, *onny onny* . . . I looked around wildly, almost panic-stricken, but then caught sight of some crooked lettering written in the dust of the floor. *Went to get supplies. Be back soon. J.C.*

I sighed, and went to the pump to get a drink. The water from it was like liquid ice and it tasted funny, but it was water. I splashed some on my face and that woke me up pretty quick. I wiped my face off on Johnny's jacket and sat down on the back steps. The hill the church was on dropped off suddenly about twenty feet from the back door, and you could see for miles and miles. It was like sitting on the top of the world.

When you haven't got anything to do, you remember things in spite of yourself. I could remember every detail of the whole night, but it had the unreal quality of a dream. It seemed much longer than twenty-four hours since Johnny and I had met Dally at the corner of Pickett and Sutton. Maybe it was. Maybe Johnny had been gone a whole week and I had just slept. Maybe he had already been worked over by the fuzz and was waiting to get the electric chair since he wouldn't tell where I was. Maybe Dally had been killed in a car wreck or something and no one would ever know where I was, and I'd just die up here, alone, and turn into a skeleton. My over-active imagination was running away with me again. Sweat ran down my face and back, and I was trembling. My head swam, and I leaned back and closed my eyes. I guess it was partly delayed shock. Finally my stomach calmed down and I relaxed a little, hoping that Johnny would remember cigarettes. I was scared, sitting there by myself.

I heard someone coming up through the dead leaves toward the back of the church, and I ducked inside the door. Then I heard a whistle, long and low, ending in a sudden high note. I knew that whistle well enough. It was used by us and the Shepard gang for "Who's there?" I returned it carefully, then darted out the door so fast that I fell off the steps and sprawled flat under Johnny's nose.

I propped myself on my elbows and grinned up at him. "Hey, Johnny. Fancy meetin' you here."

He looked down at me over a big package. "I swear, Ponyboy, you're gettin' to act more like Two-Bit every day."

I tried unsuccessfully to cock an eyebrow. "Who's acting?" I rolled over and sprang up, happy that someone was there. "What'd you get?"

"Come on inside. Dally told us to stay inside."

We went in. Johnny dusted off a table with his jacket and started taking things out of the sack and lining them up neatly. "A week's supply of baloney, two loaves of bread, a box of matches . . ." Johnny went on.

I got tired of watching him do it all, so I started digging into the sack myself. "Wheee!" I sat down on a dusty chair and stared. "A paperback copy of *Gone with the Wind*! How'd you know I always wanted one?"

Johnny reddened. "I remembered you sayin' something about it once. And me and you went to see that movie, 'member? I thought you could maybe read it out loud and help kill time or something."

"Gee, thanks." I put the book down reluctantly. I wanted to start it right then. "Peroxide? A deck of cards . . ." Suddenly I realized something. "Johnny, you ain't thinking of . . ."

Johnny sat down and pulled out his knife. "We're gonna cut our hair, and you're gonna bleach yours." He looked at the ground carefully. "They'll have our descriptions in the paper. We can't fit 'em."

"Oh, no!" My hand flew to my hair. "No, Johnny, not my hair!"

It was my pride. It was long and silky, just like Soda's, only a little redder. Our hair was tuff—we didn't have to use much grease on it. Our hair labeled us greasers, too— it was our trademark. The one thing we were proud of. Maybe we couldn't have Corvairs or madras shirts, but we could have hair.

"We'd have to anyway if we got caught. You know the first thing the judge does is make you get a haircut."

"I don't see why," I said sourly. "Dally could just as easily mug somebody with short hair."

"I don't know either—it's just a way of trying to break us. They can't really do anything to guys like Curly Shepard or Tim; they've had about everything done to them. And they can't take anything away from them because they don't have anything in the first place. So they cut their hair."

I looked at Johnny imploringly. Johnny sighed. "I'm gonna cut mine too, and wash the grease out, but I can't bleach it. I'm too dark-skinned to look okay blond. Oh, come on, Ponyboy," he pleaded. "It'll grow back."

"Okay," I said, wide-eyed. "Get it over with."

Johnny flipped out the razor-edge of his switch, took hold of my hair, and started sawing on it. I shuddered. "Not too short," I begged. "Johnny, please . . ."

Finally it was over with. My hair looked funny, scattered over the floor in tufts. "It's lighter than I thought it was," I said, examining it. "Can I see what I look like now?"

"No," Johnny said slowly, staring at me. "We gotta bleach it first."

After I'd sat in the sun for fifteen minutes to dry the bleach, Johnny let me look in the old cracked mirror we'd found in a closet. I did a double take. My hair was even lighter than Sodapop's. I'd never combed it to the side like that. It just didn't look like me. It made me look younger, and scareder, too. Boy howdy, I thought, this really makes me look tuff. I look like a blasted pansy. I was miserable.

Johnny handed me the knife. He looked scared, too. "Cut the front and thin out the rest. I'll comb it back after I wash it."

"Johnny," I said tiredly, "you can't wash your hair in that freezing water in this weather. You'll get a cold."

He only shrugged. "Go ahead and cut it."

I did the best I could. He went ahead and washed it anyway, using the bar of soap he'd bought. I was glad I had had to run away with him instead of with Two-Bit or Steve or Dally. That would be one thing they'd never think of—

soap. I gave him Dally's jacket to wrap up in, and he sat shivering in the sunlight on the back steps, leaning against the door, combing his hair back. It was the first time I could see that he had eyebrows. He didn't look like Johnny. His forehead was whiter where his bangs had been; it would have been funny if we hadn't been so scared. He was still shivering with cold. "I guess," he said weakly, "I guess we're disguised."

I leaned back next to him sullenly. "I guess so."

"Oh, shoot," Johnny said with fake cheerfulness, "it's just hair."

"Shoot nothing," I snapped. "It took me a long time to get that hair just the way I wanted it. And besides, this just ain't us. It's like being in a Halloween costume we can't get out of."

"Well, we got to get used to it," Johnny said with finality. "We're in big trouble and it's our looks or us."

I started eating a candy bar. "I'm still tired," I said. To my surprise, the ground blurred and I felt tears running down my cheeks. I brushed them off hurriedly. Johnny looked as miserable as I felt.

"I'm sorry I cut your hair off, Ponyboy."

"Oh, it ain't that," I said between bites of chocolate. "I mean, not all of it. I'm just a little spooky. I really don't know what's the matter. I'm just mixed up."

"I know," Johnny said through chattering teeth as we went inside. "Things have been happening so fast . . ." I put my arm across his shoulders to warm him up.

"Two-Bit shoulda been in that little one-horse store. Man, we're in the middle of nowhere; the nearest house is two miles away. Things were layin' out wide open, just waitin' for somebody slick like Two-Bit to come and pick 'em up. He coulda walked out with half the store." He leaned back beside me, and I could feel him trembling. "Good ol' Two-Bit," he said in a quavering voice. He must have been as homesick as I was.

"Remember how he was wisecrackin' last night?" I said. "Last night . . . just last night we were walkin' Cherry and Marcia over to Two-Bit's. Just last night we were layin' in the lot, lookin' up at the stars and dreaming . . ."

"Stop it!" Johnny gasped from between clenched teeth. "Shut up about last night! I killed a kid last night. He couldn't of been over seventeen or eighteen, and I killed him. How'd you like to live with that?" He was crying. I held him like Soda had held him the day we found him lying in the lot.

"I didn't mean to," he finally blurted out, "but they were drownin' you, and I was so scared . . ." He was quiet for a minute. "There sure is a lot of blood in people."

He got up suddenly and began pacing back and forth, slapping his pockets.

"Whatta we gonna do?" I was crying by then. It was getting dark and I was cold and lonesome. I closed my eyes and leaned my head back, but the tears came anyway.

"This is my fault," Johnny said in a miserable voice. He had stopped crying when I started. "For bringin' a little thirteen-year-old kid along. You ought to go home. You can't get into any trouble. You didn't kill him."

"No!" I screamed at him. "I'm fourteen! I've been fourteen for a month! And I'm in it as much as you are. I'll stop crying in a minute . . . I can't help it."

He slumped down beside me. "I didn't mean it like

that, Ponyboy. Don't cry, Pony, we'll be okay. Don't cry . . ."
I leaned against him and bawled until I went to sleep.

I woke up late that night. Johnny was resting against the
wall and I was asleep on his shoulder. "Johnny?" I yawned.
"You awake?" I was warm and sleepy.

"Yeah," he said quietly.

"We ain't gonna cry no more, are we?"

"Nope. We're all cried out now. We're gettin' used to
the idea. We're gonna be okay now."

"That's what I thought," I said drowsily. Then for the
first time since Dally and I had sat down behind those girls
at the Nightly Double, I relaxed. We could take whatever
was coming now.

The next four or five days were the longest days I've ever
spent in my life. We killed time by reading *Gone with the
Wind* and playing poker. Johnny sure did like that book,
although he didn't know anything about the Civil War and
even less about plantations, and I had to explain a lot of it to
him. It amazed me how Johnny could get more meaning
out of some of the stuff in there than I could—I was supposed to be the deep one. Johnny had failed a year in school
and never made good grades—he couldn't grasp anything
that was shoved at him too fast, and I guess his teachers
thought he was just plain dumb. But he wasn't. He was just
a little slow to get things, and he liked to explore things once
he did get them. He was especially stuck on the Southern
gentlemen—impressed with their manners and charm.

"I bet they were cool ol' guys," he said, his eyes glowing,
after I had read the part about them riding into sure death

because they were gallant. "They remind me of Dally."

"Dally?" I said, startled. "Shoot, he ain't got any more manners than I do. And you saw how he treated those girls the other night. Soda's more like them Southern boys."

"Yeah . . . in the manners bit, and the charm, too, I guess," Johnny said slowly, "but one night I saw Dally gettin' picked up by the fuzz, and he kept real cool and calm the whole time. They was gettin' him for breakin' out the windows in the school building, and it was Two-Bit who did that. And Dally knew it. But he just took the sentence without battin' an eye or even denyin' it. That's gallant."

That was the first time I realized the extent of Johnny's hero-worship for Dally Winston. Of all of us, Dally was the one I liked least. He didn't have Soda's understanding or dash, or Two-Bit's humor, or even Darry's superman qualities. But I realized that these three appealed to me because they were like the heroes in the novels I read. Dally was real. I liked my books and clouds and sunsets. Dally was so real he scared me.

Johnny and I never went to the front of the church. You could see the front from the road, and sometimes farm kids rode their horses by on their way to the store. So we stayed in the very back, usually sitting on the steps and looking across the valley. We could see for miles; see the ribbon of highway and the small dots that were houses and cars. We couldn't watch the sunset, since the back faced east, but I loved to look at the colors of the fields and the soft shadings of the horizon.

One morning I woke up earlier than usual. Johnny and I slept huddled together for warmth—Dally had been right when he said it would get cold where we were going. Being careful not to wake Johnny up, I went to sit on the steps and smoke a cigarette. The dawn was coming then. All the lower valley was covered with mist, and sometimes little pieces of it broke off and floated away in small clouds. The sky was lighter in the east, and the horizon was a thin golden line. The clouds changed from gray to pink, and the mist was touched with gold. There was a silent moment when everything held its breath, and then the sun rose. It was beautiful.

"Golly"—Johnny's voice beside me made me jump—"that sure was pretty."

"Yeah." I sighed, wishing I had some paint to do a picture with while the sight was still fresh in my mind.

"The mist was what was pretty," Johnny said. "All gold and silver."

"Uhmmmm," I said, trying to blow a smoke ring.

"Too bad it couldn't stay like that all the time."

"Nothing gold can stay." I was remembering a poem I'd read once.

"What?"

> "Nature's first green is gold,
> Her hardest hue to hold.
> Her early leaf's a flower;
> But only so an hour.
> Then leaf subsides to leaf.
> So Eden sank to grief,
> So dawn goes down to day.
> Nothing gold can stay."

Johnny was staring at me. "Where'd you learn that? That was what I meant."

"Robert Frost wrote it. He meant more to it than I'm gettin', though." I was trying to find the meaning the poet had in mind, but it eluded me. "I always remembered it because I never quite got what he meant by it."

"You know," Johnny said slowly, "I never noticed colors and clouds and stuff until you kept reminding me about them. It seems like they were never there before." He thought for a minute. "Your family sure is funny."

"And what happens to be so funny about it?" I asked stiffly.

Johnny looked at me quickly. "I didn't mean nothing. I meant, well, Soda kinda looks like your mother did, but he acts just exactly like your father. And Darry is the spittin' image of your father, but he ain't wild and laughing all the time like he was. He acts like your mother. And you don't act like either one."

"I know," I said. "Well," I said, thinking this over, "you ain't like any of the gang. I mean, I couldn't tell Two-Bit or Steve or even Darry about the sunrise and clouds and stuff. I couldn't even remember that poem around them. I mean, they just don't dig. Just you and Sodapop. And maybe Cherry Valance."

Johnny shrugged. "Yeah," he said with a sigh. "I guess we're different."

"Shoot," I said, blowing a perfect smoke ring, "maybe *they* are."

By the fifth day I was so tired of baloney I nearly got sick every time I looked at it. We had eaten all our candy bars in the first two days. I was dying for a Pepsi. I'm what you might call a Pepsi addict. I drink them like a fiend, and going for five days without one was about to kill me. Johnny promised to get some if we ran out of supplies and had to get some more, but that didn't help me right then. I was smoking a lot more there than I usually did—I guess because it was something to do—although Johnny warned me that I would get sick smoking so much. We were careful with our cigarettes—if that old church ever caught fire there'd be no stopping it.

On the fifth day I had read up to Sherman's siege of Atlanta in *Gone with the Wind*, owed Johnny a hundred and fifty bucks from poker games, smoked two packs of Camels, and as Johnny had predicted, got sick. I hadn't eaten anything all day; and smoking on an empty stomach doesn't make you feel real great. I curled up in a corner to sleep off the smoke. I was just about asleep when I heard, as if from a great distance, a low long whistle that went off in a sudden high note. I was too sleepy to pay any attention, although Johnny didn't have any reason to be whistling like that. He was sitting on the back steps trying to read *Gone with the Wind*. I had almost decided that I had dreamed the outside world and there was nothing real but baloney sandwiches and the Civil War and the old church and the mist in the valley. It seemed to me that I had always lived in the church, or maybe lived during the Civil War and had somehow got transplanted. That shows you what a wild imagination I have.

A toe nudged me in the ribs. "Glory," said a rough but familiar voice, "he looks different with his hair like that."

I rolled over and sat up, rubbing the sleep out of my eyes and yawning. Suddenly I blinked.

"Hey, Dally!"

"Hey, Ponyboy!" He grinned down at me. "Or should I say Sleeping Beauty?"

I never thought I'd live to see the day when I would be so glad to see Dally Winston, but right then he meant one thing: contact with the outside world. And it suddenly became real and vital.

"How's Sodapop? Are the fuzz after us? Is Darry all right? Do the boys know where we are? What . . ."

"Hold on, kid," Dally broke in. "I can't answer everything at once. You two want to go get something to eat first? I skipped breakfast and I'm about starved."

"*You're* starved?" Johnny was so indignant he nearly squeaked. I remembered the baloney.

"Is it safe to go out?" I asked eagerly.

"Yep." Dally searched his shirt pocket for a cigarette, and finding none, said, "Gotta cancer stick, Johnnycake?"

Johnny tossed him a whole package.

"The fuzz won't be lookin' for you around here," Dally said, lighting up. "They think you've lit out for Texas. I've got Buck's T-bird parked down the road a little way. Goshamighty, boys, ain't you been eatin' anything?"

Johnny looked startled. "Yeah. Whatever gave you the idea we ain't?"

Dally shook his head. "You're both pale and you've lost weight. After this, get out in the sun more. You look like you've been through the mill."

I started to say "Look who's talking" but decided it would be safer not to. Dally needed a shave—a stubble of colorless beard covered his jaw—and he looked like he was the one who'd been sleeping in his clothes for a week instead of us; I knew he hadn't seen a barber in months. But it was safer not to get mouthy with Dally Winston.

"Hey, Ponyboy"—he fumbled with a piece of paper in his back pocket—"I gotta letter for you."

"A letter? Who from?"

"The President, of course, stupid. It's from Soda."

"Sodapop?" I said, bewildered. "But how did he know . . . ?"

"He came over to Buck's a couple of days ago for something and found that sweat shirt. I told him I didn't know where you were, but he didn't believe me. He gave me this letter and half his pay check to give you. Kid, you ought to see Darry. He's takin' this mighty hard . . ."

I wasn't listening. I leaned back against the side of the church and read:

> *Ponyboy,*
>
> *Well I guess you got into some trouble, huh? Darry and me nearly went nuts when you ran out like that. Darry is awful sorry he hit you. You know he didn't mean it. And then you and Johnny turned up mising and what with that dead kid in the park and Dally getting hauled into the station, well it scared us something awful. The police came by to question us and we told them as much as we could. I can't believe little old Johnny could kill somebody. I know Dally knows where you are, but you know him. He keeps his trap shut and won't tell me nothing. Darry hasn't got the slightest notion where you're at and it is nearly killing him. I wish*

you'd come back and turn your selfves in but I
guess you can't since Johnny might get hurt. You
sure are famous. You got a paragraph in the
newspaper even. Take care and say hi to Johnny
for us.

Sodapop Curtis

He could improve his spelling, I thought after reading it through three or four times. "How come you got hauled in?" I asked Dally.

"Shoot, kid"—he grinned wolfishly—"them boys at the station know me by now. I get hauled in for everything that happens in our turf. While I was there I kinda let it slip that y'all were headin' for Texas. So that's where they're lookin'."

He took a drag on his cigarette and cussed it good-naturedly for not being a Kool. Johnny listened in admiration. "You sure can cuss good, Dally."

"Sure can," Dally agreed wholeheartedly, proud of his vocabulary. "But don't you kids get to pickin' up my bad habits."

He gave me a hard rub on the head. "Kid, I swear it don't look like you with your hair all cut off. It used to look tuff. You and Soda had the coolest-lookin' hair in town."

"I know," I said sourly. "I look lousy, but don't rub it in."

"Do y'all want somethin' to eat or not?"

Johnny and I leaped up. "You'd better believe it."

"Gee," Johnny said wistfully, "it sure will be good to get into a car again."

"Well," Dally drawled, "I'll give you a ride for your money."

Dally always did like to drive fast, as if he didn't care whether he got where he was going or not, and we came down the red dirt road off Jay Mountain doing eighty-five. I like fast driving and Johnny was crazy about drag races, but we both got a little green around the gills when Dally took a corner on two wheels with the brakes screaming. Maybe it was because we hadn't been in a car for so long.

We stopped at a Dairy Queen and the first thing I got was a Pepsi. Johnny and I gorged on barbecue sandwiches and banana splits.

"Glory," Dallas said, amazed, watching us gulp the stuff down. "You don't need to make like every mouthful's your last. I got plenty of money. Take it easy, I don't want you gettin' sick on me. And I thought I was hungry!"

Johnny merely ate faster. I didn't slow down until I got a headache.

"I didn't tell y'all something," Dally said, finishing his third hamburger. "The Socs and us are having all-out warfare all over the city. That kid you killed had plenty of friends and all over town it's Soc against grease. We can't walk alone at all. I started carryin' a heater . . ."

"Dally!" I said, frightened. "You kill people with heaters!"

"Ya kill 'em with switchblades, too, don't ya, kid?" Dally said in a hard voice. Johnny gulped. "Don't worry," Dally went on, "it ain't loaded. I ain't aimin' to get picked up for murder. But it sure does help a bluff. Tim Shepard's gang and our outfit are havin' it out with the Socs tomorrow night at the vacant lot. We got hold of the president of one of their social clubs and had a war council. Yeah"—Dally sighed, and I knew he was remembering New York—"just like the good old days. If they win, things go on as usual. If we do, they stay outa our territory but good. Two-Bit got jumped a few days ago. Darry and me came along in time, but he wasn't havin' too much trouble. Two-Bit's a good fighter. Hey, I didn't tell you we got us a spy."

"A spy?" Johnny looked up from his banana split. "Who?"

"That good-lookin' broad I tried to pick up that night you killed the Soc. The redhead, Cherry what's-her-name."

Chapter 6

JOHNNY GAGGED AND I almost dropped my hot-fudge sundae. "Cherry?" we both said at the same time. "The Soc?"

"Yeah," Dally said. "She came over to the vacant lot the night Two-Bit was jumped. Shepard and some of his outfit and us were hanging around there when she drives up in her little ol' Sting Ray. That took a lot of nerve. Some of us was for jumping her then and there, her bein' the dead kid's girl and all, but Two-Bit stopped us. Man, next time I want a broad I'll pick up my own kind."

"Yeah," Johnny said slowly, and I wondered if, like me, he was remembering another voice, also tough and just deepened into manhood, saying: "Next time you want a broad, pick up your own kind . . ." It gave me the creeps.

Dally was going on: "She said she felt that the whole

mess was her fault, which it is, and that she'd keep up with what was comin' off with the Socs in the rumble and would testify that the Socs were drunk and looking for a fight and that you fought back in self-defense." He gave a grim laugh. "That little gal sure does hate me. I offered to take her over to The Dingo for a Coke and she said 'No, thank you' and told me where I could go in very polite terms."

She was afraid of loving you, I thought. So Cherry Valance, the cheerleader, Bob's girl, the Soc, was trying to help us. No, it wasn't Cherry the Soc who was helping us, it was Cherry the dreamer who watched sunsets and couldn't stand fights. It was hard to believe a Soc would help us, even a Soc that dug sunsets. Dally didn't notice. He had forgotten about it already.

"Man, this place is out of it. What do they do for kicks around here, play checkers?" Dally surveyed the scene without interest. "I ain't never been in the country before. Have you two?"

Johnny shook his head but I said, "Dad used to take us all huntin'. I've been in the country before. How'd you know about the church?"

"I got a cousin that lives around here somewheres. Tipped me off that it'd make a tuff hide-out in case of something. Hey, Ponyboy, I heard you was the best shot in the family."

"Yeah," I said. "Darry always got the most ducks, though. Him and Dad. Soda and I goofed around too much, scared most of our game away." I couldn't tell Dally that I hated to shoot things. He'd think I was soft.

"That was a good idea, I mean cuttin' your hair and

bleachin' it. They printed your descriptions in the paper but you sure wouldn't fit 'em now."

Johnny had been quietly finishing his fifth barbecue sandwich, but now he announced: "We're goin' back and turn ourselves in."

It was Dally's turn to gag. Then he swore awhile. Then he turned to Johnny and demanded: "What?"

"I said we're goin' back and turn ourselves in," Johnny repeated in a quiet voice. I was surprised but not shocked. I had thought about turning ourselves in lots of times, but apparently the whole idea was a jolt to Dallas.

"I got a good chance of bein' let off easy," Johnny said desperately, and I didn't know if it was Dally he was trying to convince or himself. "I ain't got no record with the fuzz and it was self-defense. Ponyboy and Cherry can testify to that. And I don't aim to stay in that church all my life."

That was quite a speech for Johnny. His big black eyes grew bigger than ever at the thought of going to the police station, for Johnny had a deathly fear of cops, but he went on: "We won't tell that you helped us, Dally, and we'll give you back the gun and what's left of the money and say we hitchhiked back so you won't get into trouble. Okay?"

Dally was chewing the corner of his ID card, which gave his age as twenty-one so he could buy liquor. "You sure you want to go back? Us greasers get it worse than anyone else."

Johnny nodded. "I'm sure. It ain't fair for Ponyboy to have to stay up in that church with Darry and Soda worryin' about him all the time. I don't guess . . ."—he swallowed and tried not to look eager—"I don't guess my parents are worried about me or anything?"

"The boys are worried," Dally said in a matter-of-fact voice. "Two-Bit was going to Texas to hunt for you."

"My parents," Johnny repeated doggedly, "did they ask about me?"

"No," snapped Dally, "they didn't. Blast it, Johnny, what do they matter? Shoot, my old man don't give a hang whether I'm in jail or dead in a car wreck or drunk in the gutter. That don't bother me none."

Johnny didn't say anything. But he stared at the dashboard with such hurt bewilderment that I could have bawled.

Dally cussed under his breath and nearly tore out the transmission of the T-bird as we roared out of the Dairy Queen. I felt sorry for Dally. He meant it when he said he didn't care about his parents. But he and the rest of the gang knew Johnny cared and did everything they could to make it up to him. I don't know what it was about Johnny—maybe that lost-puppy look and those big scared eyes were what made everyone his big brother. But they couldn't, no matter how hard they tried, take the place of his parents. I thought about it for a minute—Darry and Sodapop were my brothers and I loved both of them, even if Darry did scare me; but not even Soda could take Mom and Dad's place. And they were my real brothers, not just sort of adopted ones. No wonder Johnny was hurt because his parents didn't want him. Dally could take it—Dally was of the breed that could take anything, because he was hard and tough, and when he wasn't, he could turn hard and tough. Johnny was a good fighter and could play it cool, but he was sensitive and that isn't a good way to be when you're a greaser.

"Blast it, Johnny," Dally growled as we flew along the red road, "why didn't you think of turning yourself in five days ago? It would have saved a lot of trouble."

"I was scared," Johnny said with conviction. "I still am." He ran his finger down one of his short black sideburns. "I guess we ruined our hair for nothing, Ponyboy."

"I guess so." I was glad we were going back. I was sick of that church. I didn't care if I was bald.

Dally was scowling, and from long and painful experience I knew better than to talk to him when his eyes were blazing like that. I'd likely as not get clobbered over the head. That had happened before, just as it had happened to all the gang at one time or another. We rarely fought among ourselves—Darry was the unofficial leader, since he kept his head best, Soda and Steve had been best friends since grade school and never fought, and Two-Bit was just too lazy to argue with anyone. Johnny kept his mouth shut too much to get into arguments, and nobody ever fought with Johnny. I kept my mouth shut, too. But Dally was a different matter. If something beefed him, he didn't keep quiet about it, and if you rubbed him the wrong way—look out. Not even Darry wanted to tangle with him. He was dangerous.

Johnny just sat there and stared at his feet. He hated for any one of us to be mad at him. He looked awful sad. Dally glanced at him out of the corner of his eye. I looked out the window.

"Johnny," Dally said in a pleading, high voice, using a tone I had never heard from him before, "Johnny, I ain't mad at you. I just don't want you to get hurt. You don't know what a few months in jail can do to you. Oh, blast it,

Johnny"—he pushed his white-blond hair back out of his eyes—"you get hardened in jail. I don't want that to happen to you. Like it happened to me . . ."

I kept staring out the window at the rapidly passing scenery, but I felt my eyes getting round. Dally never talked like that. Never. Dally didn't give a Yankee dime about anyone but himself, and he was cold and hard and mean. He never talked about his past or being in jail that way—if he talked about it at all, it was to brag. And I suddenly thought of Dally . . . in jail at the age of ten . . . Dally growing up in the streets . . .

"Would you rather have me living in hide-outs for the rest of my life, always on the run?" Johnny asked seriously.

If Dally had said yes, Johnny would have gone back to the church without hesitation. He figured Dally knew more than he did, and Dally's word was law. But he never heard Dally's answer, for we had reached the top of Jay Mountain and Dally suddenly slammed on the brakes and stared. "Oh, glory!" he whispered. The church was on fire!

"Let's go see what the deal is," I said, hopping out.

"What for?" Dally sounded irritated. "Get back in here before I beat your head in."

I knew Dally would have to park the car and catch me before he could carry out his threat, and Johnny was already out and following me, so I figured I was safe. We could hear him cussing us out, but he wasn't mad enough to come after us. There was a crowd at the front of the church, mostly little kids, and I wondered how they'd gotten there so quickly. I tapped the nearest grownup. "What's going on?"

"Well, we don't know for sure," the man said with a

good-natured grin. "We were having a school picnic up here and the first thing we knew, the place is burning up. Thank goodness this is a wet season and the old thing is worthless anyway." Then, to the kids, he shouted, "Stand back, children. The firemen will be coming soon."

"I bet we started it," I said to Johnny. "We must have dropped a lighted cigarette or something."

About that time a lady came running up. "Jerry, some of the kids are missing."

"They're probably around here somewhere. You can't tell with all this excitement where they might be."

"No." She shook her head. "They've been missing for at least a half an hour. I thought they were climbing the hill . . ."

Then we all froze. Faintly, just faintly, you could hear someone yelling. And it sounded like it was coming from inside the church.

The woman went white. "I told them not to play in the church . . . I told them . . ." She looked like she was going to start screaming, so Jerry shook her.

"I'll get them, don't worry!" I started at a dead run for the church, and the man caught my arm. "I'll get them. You kids stay out!"

I jerked loose and ran on. All I could think was: We started it. We started it. We started it!

I wasn't about to go through that flaming door, so I slammed a big rock through a window and pulled myself in. It was a wonder I didn't cut myself to death, now that I think about it.

"Hey, Ponyboy."

I looked around, startled. I hadn't realized Johnny had

been right behind me all the way. I took a deep breath, and started coughing. The smoke filled my eyes and they started watering. "Is that guy coming?"

Johnny shook his head. "The window stopped him."

"Too scared?"

"Naw . . ." Johnny gave me a grin. "Too fat."

I couldn't laugh because I was scared I'd drown in the smoke. The roar and crackling was getting louder, and Johnny shouted the next question.

"Where's the kids?"

"In the back, I guess," I hollered, and we started stumbling through the church. I should be scared, I thought with an odd detached feeling, but I'm not. The cinders and embers began falling on us, stinging and smarting like ants. Suddenly, in the red glow and the haze, I remembered wondering what it was like in a burning ember, and I thought: Now I know, it's a red hell. Why aren't I scared?

We pushed open the door to the back room and found four or five little kids, about eight years old or younger, huddled in a corner. One was screaming his head off, and Johnny yelled, "Shut up! We're goin' to get you out!" The kid looked surprised and quit hollering. I blinked myself— Johnny wasn't behaving at all like his old self. He looked over his shoulder and saw that the door was blocked by flames, then pushed open the window and tossed out the nearest kid. I caught one quick look at his face; it was red-marked from falling embers and sweat-streaked, but he grinned at me. He wasn't scared either. That was the only time I can think of when I saw him without that defeated, suspicious look in his eyes. He looked like he was having the time of his life.

I picked up a kid, and he promptly bit me, but I leaned out the window and dropped him as gently as I could, being in a hurry like that. A crowd was there by that time. Dally was standing there, and when he saw me he screamed, "For Pete's sake, get outa there! That roof's gonna cave in any minute. Forget those blasted kids!"

I didn't pay any attention, although pieces of the old roof were crashing down too close for comfort. I snatched up another kid, hoping he didn't bite, and dropped him without waiting to see if he landed okay or not. I was coughing so hard I could hardly stand up, and I wished I had time to take off Dally's jacket. It was hot. We dropped the last of the kids out as the front of the church started to crumble. Johnny shoved me toward the window. "Get out!"

I leaped out the window and heard timber crashing and the flames roaring right behind me. I staggered, almost falling, coughing and sobbing for breath. Then I heard Johnny scream, and as I turned to go back for him, Dally swore at me and clubbed me across the back as hard as he could, and I went down into a peaceful darkness.

When I came to, I was being bounced around, and I ached and smarted, and wondered dimly where I was. I tried to think but there was a high-pitched screaming going on, and I couldn't tell whether it was inside my head or out. Then I realized it was a siren. The fuzz, I thought dully. The cops have come for us. I tried to swallow a groan and wished wildly for Soda. Someone with a cold wet rag was gently sponging off my face, and a voice said, "I think he's coming around."

I opened my eyes. It was dark. I'm moving, I thought. Are they taking me to jail?

"Where . . . ?" I said hoarsely, not able to get anything else out of my mouth. My throat was sore. I blinked at the stranger sitting beside me. But he wasn't a stranger . . . I'd seen him before . . .

"Take it easy, kid. You're in an ambulance."

"Where's Johnny?" I cried, frightened at being in this car with strangers. "And Dallas?"

"They're in the other ambulance, right behind us. Just calm down. You're going to be okay. You just passed out."

"I didn't either," I said in the bored, tough voice we reserved for strangers and cops. "Dallas hit me. How come?"

"Because your back was in flames, that's why."

I was surprised. "It was? Golly, I didn't feel it. It don't hurt."

"We put it out before you got burned. That jacket saved you from a bad burning, maybe saved your life. You just keeled over from smoke inhalation and a little shock—of course, that slap on the back didn't help much."

I remembered who he was then—Jerry somebody-or-other who was too heavy to get in the window. He must be a school teacher, I thought. "Are you taking us to the police station?" I was still a little mixed up as to what was coming off.

"The police station?" It was his turn to be surprised. "What would we want to take you to the police station for? We're taking all three of you to the hospital."

I let his first remark slide by. "Are Johnny and Dally all right?"

"Which one's which?"

"Johnny has black hair. Dally's the mean-looking one."

He studied his wedding ring. Maybe he's thinking about his wife, I thought. I wished he'd say something.

"We think the towheaded kid is going to be all right. He burned one arm pretty badly, though, trying to drag the other kid out the window. Johnny, well, I don't know about him. A piece of timber caught him across the back—he might have a broken back, and he was burned pretty severely. He passed out before he got out the window. They're giving him plasma now." He must have seen the look on my face because he hurriedly changed the subject. "I swear, you three are the bravest kids I've seen in a long time. First you and the black-haired kid climbing in that window, and then the tough-looking kid going back in to save him. Mrs. O'Briant and I think you were sent straight from heaven. Or are you just professional heroes or something?"

Sent from heaven? Had he gotten a good look at Dallas? "No, we're greasers," I said. I was too worried and scared to appreciate the fact that he was trying to be funny.

"You're what?"

"Greasers. You know, like hoods, JD's. Johnny is wanted for murder, and Dallas has a record with the fuzz a mile long."

"Are you kidding me?" Jerry stared at me as if he thought I was still in shock or something.

"I am not. Take me to town and you'll find out pretty quick."

"We're taking you to a hospital there anyway. The address card in your billfold said that was where you lived. Your name's really Ponyboy?"

"Yeah. Even on my birth certificate. And don't bug me about it. Are . . ."—I felt weak—"are the little kids okay?"

"Just fine. A little frightened maybe. There were some short explosions right after you all got out. Sounded just exactly like gunfire."

Gunfire. There went our gun. And *Gone with the Wind*. Were we sent from heaven? I started to laugh weakly. I guess that guy knew how close to hysterics I really was, for he talked to me in a low soothing voice all the way to the hospital.

I was sitting in the waiting room, waiting to hear how Dally and Johnny were. I had been checked over, and except for a few burns and a big bruise across my back, I was all right. I had watched them bring Dally and Johnny in on stretchers. Dally's eyes were closed, but when I spoke he had tried to grin and had told me that if I ever did a stupid thing like that again he'd beat the tar out of me. He was still swearing at me when they took him on in. Johnny was unconscious. I had been afraid to look at him, but I was relieved to see that his face wasn't burned. He just looked very pale and still and sort of sick. I would have cried at the sight of him so still except I couldn't in front of people.

Jerry Wood had stayed with me all the time. He kept thanking me for getting the kids out. He didn't seem to mind our being hoods. I told him the whole story—starting when Dallas and Johnny and I had met at the corner of Pickett and Sutton. I left out the part about the gun and our hitching a ride in the freight car. He was real nice about it and said that being heroes would help get us out of trouble, especially since it was self-defense and all.

I was sitting there, smoking a cigarette, when Jerry came back in from making a phone call. He stared at me for a second. "You shouldn't be smoking."

I was startled. "How come?" I looked at my cigarette. It looked okay to me. I looked around for a "No Smoking" sign and couldn't find one. "How come?"

"Why, uh," Jerry stammered, "uh, you're too young."

"I am?" I had never thought about it. Everyone in our neighborhood, even the girls, smoked. Except for Darry, who was too proud of his athletic health to risk a cigarette, we had all started smoking at an early age. Johnny had been smoking since he was nine; Steve started at eleven. So no one thought it unusual when I started. I was the weed-fiend in my family—Soda smokes only to steady his nerves or when he wants to look tough.

Jerry simply sighed, then grinned. "There are some people here to see you. Claim to be your brothers or something."

I leaped up and ran for the door, but it was already open and Soda had me in a bear hug and was swinging me around. I was so glad to see him I could have bawled. Finally he set me down and looked at me. He pushed my hair back. "Oh, Ponyboy, your hair . . . your tuff, tuff hair . . ."

Then I saw Darry. He was leaning in the doorway, wearing his olive jeans and black T-shirt. He was still tall, broad-shouldered Darry; but his fists were jammed in his pockets and his eyes were pleading. I simply looked at him. He swallowed and said in a husky voice, "Ponyboy . . ."

I let go of Soda and stood there for a minute. Darry didn't like me . . . he had driven me away that night . . . he had hit me . . . Darry hollered at me all the time . . . he didn't give a hang about me. . . . Suddenly I realized, horrified, that Darry was crying. He didn't make a sound, but tears were running down his cheeks. I hadn't seen him cry in years, not even when Mom and Dad had been killed. (I remembered the funeral. I had sobbed in spite of myself; Soda had broken down and bawled like a baby; but Darry had only stood there, his fists in his pockets and that look on his face, the same helpless, pleading look that he was wearing now.)

In that second what Soda and Dally and Two-Bit had been trying to tell me came through. Darry did care about me, maybe as much as he cared about Soda, and because he cared he was trying too hard to make something of me. When he yelled "Pony, where have you been all this time?" he meant "Pony, you've scared me to death. Please be careful, because I couldn't stand it if anything happened to you."

Darry looked down and turned away silently. Suddenly I broke out of my daze.

"Darry!" I screamed, and the next thing I knew I had him around the waist and was squeezing the daylights out of him.

"Darry," I said, "I'm sorry . . ."

He was stroking my hair and I could hear the sobs racking him as he fought to keep back the tears. "Oh, Pony, I thought we'd lost you . . . like we did Mom and Dad . . ."

That was his silent fear then—of losing another person he loved. I remembered how close he and Dad had been, and I wondered how I could ever have thought him hard and unfeeling. I listened to his heart pounding through his T-shirt and knew everything was going to be okay now. I had taken the long way around, but I was finally home. To stay.

Chapter 7

Now there were three of us sitting in the waiting room waiting to hear how Dally and Johnny were. Then the reporters and the police came. They asked too many questions too fast, and got me mixed up. If you want to know the truth, I wasn't feeling real good in the first place. Kind of sick, really. And I'm scared of policemen anyway. The reporters fired one question right after another at me and got me so confused I didn't know what was coming off. Darry finally told them I wasn't in any shape to be yelled at so much and they slowed down a little. Darry's kinda big.

Sodapop kept them in stitches. He'd grab one guy's press hat and another's camera and walk around interviewing the nurses and mimicking TV reporters. He tried to lift a policeman's gun and grinned so crazily when he was caught that the policeman had to grin too. Soda can make anyone grin. I managed to get hold of some hair grease and comb my hair back so that it looked a little better before they got any pictures. I'd die if I got my picture in the paper with my hair looking so lousy. Darry and Sodapop were in the pictures too; Jerry Wood told me that if Sodapop and Darry hadn't been so good-looking, they wouldn't have taken so many. That was public appeal, he said.

Soda was really getting a kick out of all this. I guess he would have enjoyed it more if it hadn't been so serious, but he couldn't resist anything that caused that much excitement. I swear, sometimes he reminds me of a colt. A long-legged palomino colt that has to get his nose into everything. The reporters stared at him admiringly; I told you he looks like a movie star, and he kind of radiates.

Finally, even Sodapop got tired of the reporters—he gets bored with the same old thing after a time—and stretching out on the long bench, he put his head in Darry's lap and went to sleep. I guess both of them were tired—it was late at night and I knew they hadn't had much sleep during the week. Even while I was answering questions I remembered that it had been only a few hours since I was sleeping off a smoke in the corner of the church. Already it was an unreal dream and yet, at the time I couldn't have imagined any other world. Finally, the reporters started to leave, along with the police. One of them turned and asked, "What would you do right now if you could do anything you wanted?"

I looked at him tiredly. "Take a bath."

They thought that was pretty funny, but I meant it. I felt

lousy. The hospital got real quiet after they left. The only noise was the nurse's soft footsteps and Soda's light breathing. Darry looked down at him and grinned half-heartedly. "He didn't get much sleep this week," he said softly. "He hardly slept at all."

"Hhhmmmm," Soda said drowsily, "you didn't either."

The nurses wouldn't tell us anything about Johnny and Dally, so Darry got hold of the doctor. The doctor told us that he would talk only to the family, but Darry finally got it through the guy's head that we were about as much family as Dally and Johnny had.

Dally would be okay after two or three days in the hospital, he said. One arm was badly burned and would be scarred for the rest of his life, but he would have full use of it in a couple of weeks. Dally'll be okay, I thought. Dallas is always okay. He could take anything. It was Johnny I was worried about.

He was in critical condition. His back had been broken when that piece of timber fell on him. He was in severe shock and suffering from third-degree burns. They were doing everything they could to ease the pain, although since his back was broken he couldn't even feel the burns below his waist. He kept calling for Dallas and Ponyboy. If he lived . . . *If?* Please, no, I thought. Please not "if." The blood was draining from my face and Darry put an arm across my shoulder and squeezed hard. . . . Even if he lived he'd be crippled for the rest of his life. "You wanted it straight and you got it straight," the doctor said. "Now go home and get some rest."

I was trembling. A pain was growing in my throat and I wanted to cry, but greasers don't cry in front of strangers.

Some of us never cry at all. Like Dally and Two-Bit and Tim Shepard—they forgot how at an early age. Johnny crippled for life? I'm dreaming, I thought in panic, I'm dreaming. I'll wake up at home or in the church and everything'll be like it used to be. But I didn't believe myself. Even if Johnny did live he'd be crippled and never play football or help us out in a rumble again. He'd have to stay in that house he hated, where he wasn't wanted, and things could never be like they used to be. I didn't trust myself to speak. If I said one word, the hard knot in my throat would swell and I'd be crying in spite of myself.

I took a deep breath and kept my mouth shut. Soda was awake by then, and although he looked stony-faced, as if he hadn't heard a word the doctor had said, his eyes were bleak and stunned. Serious reality has a hard time coming through to Soda, but when it does, it hits him hard. He looked like I felt when I had seen that black-haired Soc lying doubled up and still in the moonlight.

Darry was rubbing the back of my head softly. "We'd better go home. We can't do anything here."

In our Ford I was suddenly overcome by sleepiness. I leaned back and closed my eyes and we were home before I knew it. Soda was shaking me gently. "Hey, Ponyboy, wake up. You still got to get to the house."

"Hmmmmm," I said sleepily, and lay down in the seat. I couldn't have gotten up to save my life. I could hear Soda and Darry, but as if from a great distance.

"Oh, come on, Ponyboy," Soda pleaded, shaking me a little harder, "we're sleepy, too."

I guess Darry was tired of fooling around, because he picked me up and carried me in.

"He's getting mighty big to be carried," Soda said. I wanted to tell him to shut up and let me sleep but I only yawned.

"He's sure lost a lot of weight," Darry said.

I thought sleepily that I should at least pull off my shoes, but I didn't. I went to sleep the minute Darry tossed me on the bed. I'd forgotten how soft a bed really was.

I was the first one up the next morning. Soda must have pulled my shoes and shirt off for me; I was still wearing my jeans. He must have been too sleepy to undress himself, though; he lay stretched out beside me fully clothed. I wiggled out from under his arm and pulled the blanket up over him, then went to take a shower. Asleep, he looked a lot younger than going-on-seventeen, but I had noticed that Johnny looked younger when he was asleep, too, so I figured everyone did. Maybe people are younger when they are asleep.

After my shower, I put on some clean clothes and spent five minutes or so hunting for a hint of beard on my face and mourning over my hair. That bum haircut made my ears stick out.

Darry was still asleep when I went into the kitchen to fix breakfast. The first one up has to fix breakfast and the other two do the dishes. That's the rule around our house, and usually it's Darry who fixes breakfast and me and Soda who are left with the dishes. I hunted through the icebox and found some eggs. We all like our eggs done differently. I like them hard, Darry likes them in a bacon-and-tomato sandwich, and Sodapop eats his with grape jelly. All three of us like chocolate cake for breakfast. Mom had never allowed it with ham and eggs, but Darry let Soda and me talk him into it. We really didn't have to twist his arm; Darry loves chocolate cake as much as we do. Sodapop always makes sure there's some in the icebox every night and if there isn't he cooks one up real quick. I like Darry's cakes better; Sodapop always puts too much sugar in the icing. I don't see how he stands jelly and eggs and chocolate cake all at once, but he seems to like it. Darry drinks black coffee, and Sodapop and I drink chocolate milk. We could have coffee if we wanted it, but we like chocolate milk. All three of us are crazy about chocolate stuff. Soda says if they ever make a chocolate cigarette I'll have it made.

"Anybody home?" a familiar voice called through the front screen, and Two-Bit and Steve came in. We always just stick our heads into each other's houses and holler "Hey" and walk in. Our front door is always unlocked in case one of the boys is hacked off at his parents and needs a place to lay over and cool off. We never could tell who we'd find stretched out on the sofa in the morning. It was usually Steve, whose father told him about once a week to get out and never come back. It kind of bugs Steve, even if his old man does give him five or six bucks the next day to make up for it. Or it might be Dally, who lived anywhere he could. Once we even found Tim Shepard, leader of the Shepard gang and far from his own turf, reading the morning paper in the armchair. He merely looked up, said "Hi," and strolled out without staying for breakfast. Two-Bit's mother warned us about burglars, but Darry, flexing his muscles so that they bulged like oversized baseballs, drawled that he wasn't afraid of any burglars, and that we didn't really have anything worth taking. He'd risk a robbery, he said, if it meant keeping one of the boys from blowing up and robbing a gas station or something. So the door was never locked.

"In here!" I yelled, forgetting that Darry and Sodapop were still asleep. "Don't slam the door."

They slammed the door, of course, and Two-Bit came running into the kitchen. He caught me by the upper arms and swung me around, ignoring the fact that I had two uncooked eggs in my hand.

"Hey, Ponyboy," he cried gleefully, "long time no see."

You would have thought it had been five years instead of five days since I'd seen him last, but I didn't mind. I like ol' Two-Bit; he's a good buddy to have. He spun me into Steve, who gave me a playful slap on my bruised back and shoved me across the room. One of the eggs went flying. It landed on the clock and I tightened my grip on the other one, so that it crushed and ran all over my hand.

"Now look what you did," I griped. "There went our breakfast. Can't you two wait till I set the eggs down before you go shovin' me all over the country?" I really was a little mad, because I had just realized how long it had been since I'd eaten anything. The last thing I'd eaten was a hot-fudge sundae at the Dairy Queen in Windrixville, and I was hungry.

Two-Bit was walking in a slow circle around me, and I sighed because I knew what was coming.

"Man, dig baldy here!" He was staring at my head as he circled me. "I wouldn't have believed it. I thought all the wild Indians in Oklahoma had been tamed. What little

squaw's got that tuff-lookin' mop of yours, Ponyboy?"

"Aw, lay off," I said. I wasn't feeling too good in the first place, kind of like I was coming down with something. Two-Bit winked at Steve, and Steve said, "Why, he had to get a haircut to get his picture in the paper. They'd never believe a greasy-lookin' mug could be a hero. How do you like bein' a hero, big shot?"

"How do I like *what?*"

"Being a hero. You know"—he shoved the morning paper at me impatiently—"like a big shot, even."

I stared at the newspaper. On the front page of the second section was the headline: JUVENILE DELINQUENTS TURN HEROES.

"What I like is the 'turn' bit," Two-Bit said, cleaning the egg up off the floor. "Y'all were heroes from the beginning. You just didn't 'turn' all of a sudden."

I hardly heard him. I was reading the paper. That whole page was covered with stories about us—the fight, the murder, the church burning, the Socs being drunk, everything. My picture was there, with Darry and Sodapop. The article told how Johnny and I had risked our lives saving those little kids, and there was a comment from one of the parents, who said that they would all have burned to death if it hadn't been for us. It told the whole story of our fight with the Socs—only they didn't say "Socs," because most grownups don't know about the battles that go on between us. They had interviewed Cherry Valance, and she said Bob had been drunk and that the boys had been looking for a fight when they took her home. Bob had told her he'd fix us for picking up his girl. His buddy Randy Adderson, who had helped jump us, also said it was their fault and that we'd

only fought back in self-defense. But they were charging Johnny with manslaughter. Then I discovered that I was supposed to appear at juvenile court for running away, and Johnny was too, if he recovered. (Not *if*, I thought again. Why do they keep saying *if?*) For once, there weren't any charges against Dally, and I knew he'd be mad because the paper made him out a hero for saving Johnny and didn't say much about his police record, which he was kind of proud of. He'd kill those reporters if he got hold of them. There was another column about just Darry and Soda and me: how Darry worked on two jobs at once and made good at both of them, and about his outstanding record at school; it mentioned Sodapop dropping out of school so we could stay together, and that I made the honor roll at school all the time and might be a future track star. (Oh, yeah, I forgot—I'm on the A-squad track team, the youngest one. I'm a good runner.) Then it said we shouldn't be separated after we had worked so hard to stay together.

The meaning of that last line finally hit me. "You mean . . ."—I swallowed hard—"that they're thinking about putting me and Soda in a boys' home or something?"

Steve was carefully combing back his hair in complicated swirls. "Somethin' like that."

I sat down in a daze. We couldn't get hauled off now. Not after me and Darry had finally got through to each other, and now that the big rumble was coming up and we would settle this Soc-greaser thing once and for all. Not now, when Johnny needed us and Dally was still in the hospital and wouldn't be out for the rumble.

"No," I said out loud, and Two-Bit, who was scraping the egg off the clock, turned to stare at me.

"No what?"

"No, they ain't goin' to put us in a boys' home."

"Don't worry about it," Steve said, cocksure that he and Sodapop could handle anything that came up. "They don't do things like that to heroes. Where're Soda and Superman?"

That was as far as he got, because Darry, shaved and dressed, came in behind Steve and lifted him up off the floor, then dropped him. We all call Darry "Superman" or "Muscles" at one time or another; but one time Steve made the mistake of referring to him as "all brawn and no brain," and Darry almost shattered Steve's jaw. Steve didn't call him that again, but Darry never forgave him; Darry has never really gotten over not going to college. That was the only time I've ever seen Soda mad at Steve, although Soda attaches no importance to education. School bored him. No action.

Soda came running in. "Where's that blue shirt I washed yesterday?" He took a swig of chocolate milk out of the container.

"Hate to tell you, buddy," Steve said, still flat on the floor, "but you have to wear clothes to work. There's a law or something."

"Oh, yeah," Soda said. "Where're those wheat jeans, too?"

"I ironed. They're in my closet," Darry said. "Hurry up, you're gonna be late."

Soda ran back, muttering, "I'm hurryin', I'm hurryin'."

Steve followed him and in a second there was the general racket of a pillow fight. I absent-mindedly watched Darry as he searched the icebox for chocolate cake.

"Darry," I said suddenly, "did you know about the juvenile court?"

Without turning to look at me he said evenly, "Yeah, the cops told me last night."

I knew then that he realized we might get separated. I didn't want to worry him any more, but I said, "I had one of those dreams last night. The one I can't ever remember."

Darry spun around to face me, genuine fear on his face. "What?"

I had a nightmare the night of Mom and Dad's funeral. I'd had nightmares and wild dreams every once in a while when I was little, but nothing like this one. I woke up screaming bloody murder. And I never could remember what it was that had scared me. It scared Sodapop and Darry almost as bad as it scared me; for night after night, for weeks on end, I would dream this dream and wake up in a cold sweat or screaming. And I never could remember exactly what happened in it. Soda began sleeping with me, and it stopped recurring so often, but it happened often enough for Darry to take me to a doctor. The doctor said I had too much imagination. He had a simple cure, too: Study harder, read more, draw more, and play football more. After a hard game of football and four or five hours of reading, I was too exhausted, mentally and physically, to dream anything. But Darry never got over it, and every once in a while he would ask me if I ever dreamed any more.

"Was it very bad?" Two-Bit questioned. He knew the whole story, and having never dreamed about anything but blondes, he was interested.

"No," I lied. I had awakened in a cold sweat and shivering, but Soda was dead to the world. I had just wiggled closer to him and stayed awake for a couple of hours, trembling under his arm. That dream always scared the heck out of me.

Darry started to say something, but before he could begin, Sodapop and Steve came in.

"You know what?" Sodapop said to no one in particular. "When we stomp the Socies good, me and Stevie here are gonna throw a big party and everybody can get stoned. Then we'll go chase the Socs clear to Mexico."

"Where you gonna get the dough, little man?" Darry had found the cake and was handing out pieces.

"I'll think of somethin'," Sodapop assured him between bites.

"You going to take Sandy to the party?" I asked, just to be saying something. Instant silence. I looked around. "What's the deal?"

Sodapop was staring at his feet, but his ears were reddening. "No. She went to live with her grandmother in Florida."

"How come?"

"Look," Steve said, surprisingly angry, "does he have to draw you a picture? It was either that or get married, and her parents almost hit the roof at the idea of her marryin' a sixteen-year-old kid."

"Seventeen," Soda said softly. "I'll be seventeen in a couple of weeks."

"Oh," I said, embarrassed. Soda was no innocent; I had been in on bull sessions and his bragging was as loud as anyone's. But never about Sandy. Not ever about Sandy. I remembered how her blue eyes had glowed when she looked at him, and I was sorry for her.

There was a heavy silence. Then Darry said, "We'd better get on to work, Pepsi-Cola." Darry rarely called Soda by Dad's pet nickname for him, but he did so then because he knew how miserable Sodapop was about Sandy.

"I hate to leave you here by yourself, Ponyboy," Darry said slowly. "Maybe I ought to take the day off."

"I've stayed by my lonesome before. You can't afford a day off."

"Yeah, but you just got back and I really ought to stay . . ."

"I'll baby-sit him," Two-Bit said, ducking as I took a swing at him. "I haven't got anything better to do."

"Why don't you get a job?" Steve said. "Ever consider working for a living?"

"Work?" Two-Bit was aghast. "And ruin my rep? I wouldn't be baby-sittin' the kid here if I knew of some good day-nursery open on Saturdays."

I pulled his chair over backward and jumped on him, but he had me down in a second. I was kind of short on wind. I've got to cut out smoking or I won't make track next year.

"Holler uncle."

"Nope," I said, struggling, but I didn't have my usual strength.

Darry was pulling on his jacket. "You two do up the dishes. You can go to the movies if you want to before you go see Dally and Johnny." He paused for a second, watching Two-Bit squash the heck out of me. "Two-Bit, lay off. He ain't lookin' so good. Ponyboy, you take a couple of aspirins and go easy. You smoke more than a pack today and I'll skin you. Understood?"

"Yeah," I said, getting to my feet. "You carry more than one bundle of roofing at a time today and me and Soda'll skin you. Understood?"

He grinned one of his rare grins. "Yeah. See y'all this afternoon."

"Bye," I said. I heard our Ford's *vvrrrrooooom* and thought: Soda's driving. And they left.

". . . anyway, I was walking around downtown and started to take this short cut through an alley"—Two-Bit was telling me about one of his many exploits while we did the dishes. I mean, while I did the dishes. He was sitting on the cabinet, sharpening that black-handled switchblade he was so proud of—". . . and I ran into three guys. I says 'Howdy' and they just look at each other. Then one says 'We would jump you but since you're as slick as us we figger you don't have nothin' worth takin'.' I says 'Buddy, that's the truth' and went right on. Moral: What's the safest thing to be when one is met by a gang of social outcasts in an alley?"

"A judo expert?" I suggested.

"No, another social outcast!" Two-Bit yelped, and nearly fell off the cabinet from laughing so hard. I had to grin, too. He saw things straight and made them into something funny.

"We're gonna clean up the house," I said. "The reporters or police or somebody might come by, and anyway, it's time for those guys from the state to come by and check up on us."

"This house ain't messy. You oughtta see my house."

"I have. And if you had the sense of a billy goat you'd try to help around your place instead of bumming around."

"Shoot, kid, if I ever did that my mom would die of shock."

I liked Two-Bit's mother. She had the same good humor and easygoing ways that he did. She wasn't lazy like him, but she let him get away with murder. I don't know, though—it's just about impossible to get mad at him.

When we had finished, I pulled on Dally's brown leather jacket—the back was burned black—and we started for Tenth Street.

"I would drive us," Two-Bit said as we walked up the street trying to thumb a ride, "but the brakes are out on my car. Almost killed me and Kathy the other night." He flipped the collar of his black leather jacket up to serve as a windbreak while he lit a cigarette. "You oughtta see Kathy's brother. Now there's a hood. He's so greasy he glides when he walks. He goes to the barber for an oil change, not a haircut."

I would have laughed, but I had a terrific headache. We stopped at the Tasty Freeze to buy Cokes and rest up, and the blue Mustang that had been trailing us for eight blocks pulled in. I almost decided to run, and Two-Bit must have guessed this, for he shook his head ever so slightly and tossed me a cigarette. As I lit up, the Socs who had jumped Johnny and me at the park hopped out of the Mustang. I recognized Randy Adderson, Marcia's boyfriend, and the tall guy that had almost drowned me. I hated them. It was their fault Bob was dead; their fault Johnny was dying; their fault Soda and I might get put in a boys' home. I hated them as bitterly and as contemptuously as Dally Winston hated.

Two-Bit put an elbow on my shoulder and leaned against me, dragging on his cigarette. "You know the rules. No jazz before the rumble," he said to the Socs.

"We know," Randy said. He looked at me. "Come here. I want to talk to you."

I glanced at Two-Bit. He shrugged. I followed Randy over to his car, out of earshot of the rest. We sat there in his car for a second, silent. Golly, that was the tuffest car I've ever been in.

"I read about you in the paper," Randy said finally. "How come?"

"I don't know. Maybe I felt like playing hero."

"I wouldn't have. I would have let those kids burn to death."

"You might not have. You might have done the same thing."

Randy pulled out a cigarette and pressed in the car lighter. "I don't know. I don't know anything anymore. I would never have believed a greaser could pull something like that."

"'Greaser' didn't have anything to do with it. My buddy over there wouldn't have done it. Maybe you would have done the same thing, maybe a friend of yours wouldn't have. It's the individual."

"I'm not going to show at the rumble tonight," Randy said slowly.

I took a good look at him. He was seventeen or so, but he was already old. Like Dallas was old. Cherry had said her friends were too cool to feel anything, and yet she

could remember watching sunsets. Randy was supposed to
be too cool to feel anything, and yet there was pain in his
eyes.

"I'm sick of all this. Sick and tired. Bob was a good guy.
He was the best buddy a guy ever had. I mean, he was a
good fighter and tuff and everything, but he was a real person too. You dig?"

I nodded.

"He's dead—his mother has had a nervous breakdown.
They spoiled him rotten. I mean, most parents would be
proud of a kid like that—good-lookin' and smart and
everything, but they gave in to him all the time. He kept
trying to make someone say 'No' and they never did. They
never did. That was what he wanted. For somebody to tell
him 'No.' To have somebody lay down the law, set the lim-
its, give him something solid to stand on. That's what we
all want, really. One time . . ."—Randy tried to grin, but I
could tell he was close to tears—"one time he came home
drunker than anything. He thought sure they were gonna
raise the roof. You know what they did? They thought
it was something *they'd* done. They thought it was their
fault—that they'd failed him and driven him to it or something. They took all the blame and didn't do anything to
him. If his old man had just belted him—just once, he
might still be alive. I don't know why I'm telling you this. I
couldn't tell anyone else. My friends—they'd think I was
off my rocker or turning soft. Maybe I am. I just know that
I'm sick of this whole mess. That kid—your buddy, the
one that got burned—he might die?"

"Yeah," I said, trying not to think about Johnny.

"And tonight . . . people get hurt in rumbles, maybe

killed. I'm sick of it because it doesn't do any good. You can't win, you know that, don't you?" And when I remained silent he went on: "You can't win, even if you whip us. You'll still be where you were before—at the bottom. And we'll still be the lucky ones with all the breaks. So it doesn't do any good, the fighting and the killing. It doesn't prove a thing. We'll forget it if you win, or if you don't. Greasers will still be greasers and Socs will still be Socs. Sometimes I think it's the ones in the middle that are really the lucky stiffs . . ." He took a deep breath. "So I'd fight if I thought it'd do any good. I think I'm going to leave town. Take my little old Mustang and all the dough I can carry and get out."

"Running away won't help."

"Oh, hell, I know it," Randy half-sobbed, "but what can I do? I'm marked chicken if I punk out at the rumble, and I'd hate myself if I didn't. I don't know what to do."

"I'd help you if I could," I said. I remembered Cherry's voice: *Things are rough all over.* I knew then what she meant.

He looked at me. "No, you wouldn't. I'm a Soc. You get a little money and the whole world hates you."

"No," I said, "you hate the whole world."

He just looked at me—from the way he looked he could have been ten years older than he was. I got out of the car. "You would have saved those kids if you had been there," I said. "You'd have saved them the same as we did."

"Thanks, grease," he said, trying to grin. Then he stopped. "I didn't mean that. I meant, thanks, kid."

"My name's Ponyboy," I said. "Nice talkin' to you, Randy."

I walked over to Two-Bit, and Randy honked for his friends to come and get into the car.

"What'd he want?" Two-Bit asked. "What'd Mr. Super-Soc have to say?"

"He ain't a Soc," I said, "he's just a guy. He just wanted to talk."

"You want to see a movie before we go see Johnny and Dallas?"

"Nope," I said, lighting up another weed. I still had a headache, but I felt better. Socs were just guys after all. Things were rough all over, but it was better that way. That way you could tell the other guy was human too.

Chapter 8

THE NURSES WOULDN'T let us see Johnny. He was in critical condition. No visitors. But Two-Bit wouldn't take no for an answer. That was his buddy in there and he aimed to see him. We both begged and pleaded, but we were getting nowhere until the doctor found out what was going on.

"Let them go in," he said to the nurse. "He's been asking for them. It can't hurt now."

Two-Bit didn't notice the expression in his voice. It's true, I thought numbly, he is dying. We went in, practically on tiptoe, because the quietness of the hospital scared us. Johnny was lying still, with his eyes closed, but when Two-Bit said, "Hey, Johnnykid," he opened them and looked at us, trying to grin. "Hey, y'all."

The nurse, who was pulling the shades open, smiled and said, "So he can talk after all."

Two-Bit looked around. "They treatin' you okay, kid?"

"Don't . . ."—Johnny gasped—"don't let me put enough grease on my hair."

"Don't talk," Two-Bit said, pulling up a chair, "just listen. We'll bring you some hair grease next time. We're havin' the big rumble tonight."

Johnny's huge black eyes widened a little, but he didn't say anything.

"It's too bad you and Dally can't be in it. It's the first big rumble we've had—not countin' the time we whipped Shepard's outfit."

"He came by," Johnny said.

"Tim Shepard?"

Johnny nodded. "Came to see Dally."

Tim and Dallas had always been buddies.

"Did you know you got your name in the paper for being a hero?"

Johnny almost grinned as he nodded. "Tuff enough," he managed, and by the way his eyes were glowing, I figured Southern gentlemen had nothing on Johnny Cade.

I could see that even a few words were tiring him out; he was as pale as the pillow and looked awful. Two-Bit pretended not to notice.

"You want anything besides hair grease, kid?"

Johnny barely nodded. "The book"—he looked at me—"can you get another one?"

Two-Bit looked at me too. I hadn't told him about *Gone with the Wind*.

"He wants a copy of *Gone with the Wind* so I can read it

to him," I explained. "You want to run down to the drug-store and get one?"

"Okay," Two-Bit said cheerfully. "Don't y'all run off."

I sat down in Two-Bit's chair and tried to think of something to say. "Dally's gonna be okay," I said finally. "And Darry and me, we're okay now."

I knew Johnny understood what I meant. We had always been close buddies, and those lonely days in the church strengthened our friendship. He tried to smile again, and then suddenly went white and closed his eyes tight.

"Johnny!" I said, alarmed. "Are you okay?"

He nodded, keeping his eyes closed. "Yeah, it just hurts sometimes. It usually don't . . . I can't feel anything below the middle of my back . . ."

He lay breathing heavily for a moment. "I'm pretty bad off, ain't I, Pony?"

"You'll be okay," I said with fake cheerfulness. "You gotta be. We couldn't get along without you."

The truth of that last statement hit me. We couldn't get along without him. We needed Johnny as much as he needed the gang. And for the same reason.

"I won't be able to walk again," Johnny started, then faltered. "Not even on crutches. Busted my back."

"You'll be okay," I repeated firmly. Don't start crying, I commanded myself, don't start crying, you'll scare Johnny.

"You want to know something, Ponyboy? I'm scared stiff. I used to talk about killing myself . . ." He drew a quivering breath. "I don't want to die now. It ain't long enough. Sixteen years ain't long enough. I wouldn't mind it so much if there wasn't so much stuff I ain't done yet and so many things I ain't seen. It's not fair. You know what? That

time we were in Windrixville was the only time I've been
away from our neighborhood."

"You ain't gonna die," I said, trying to hold my voice
down. "And don't get juiced up, because the doc won't let
us see you no more if you do."

Sixteen years on the streets and you can learn a lot. But
all the wrong things, not the things you want to learn.
Sixteen years on the streets and you see a lot. But all the
wrong sights, not the sights you want to see.

Johnny closed his eyes and rested quietly for a minute.
Years of living on the East Side teaches you how to shut off
your emotions. If you didn't, you would explode. You learn
to cool it.

A nurse appeared in the doorway. "Johnny," she said
quietly, "your mother's here to see you."

Johnny opened his eyes. At first they were wide with
surprise, then they darkened. "I don't want to see her," he
said firmly.

"She's your mother."

"I said I don't want to see her." His voice was rising.
"She's probably come to tell me about all the trouble I'm
causing her and about how glad her and the old man'll be
when I'm dead. Well, tell her to leave me alone. For once"
—his voice broke—"for once just to leave me alone." He
was struggling to sit up, but he suddenly gasped, went
whiter than the pillowcase, and passed out cold.

The nurse hurried me out the door. "I was afraid of
something like this if he saw anyone."

I ran into Two-Bit, who was coming in.

"You can't see him now," the nurse said, so Two-Bit
handed her the book. "Make sure he can see it when he

comes around." She took it and closed the door behind her. Two-Bit stood and looked at the door a long time. "I wish it was any one of us except Johnny," he said, and his voice was serious for once. "We could get along without anyone but Johnny."

Turning abruptly, he said, "Let's go see Dallas."

As we walked out into the hall, we saw Johnny's mother. I knew her. She was a little woman, with straight black hair and big black eyes like Johnny's. But that was as far as the resemblance went. Johnnycake's eyes were fearful and sensitive; hers were cheap and hard. As we passed her she was saying, "But I have a right to see him. He's my son. After all the trouble his father and I've gone to to raise him, this is our reward! He'd rather see those no-count hoodlums than his own folks . . ." She saw us and gave us such a look of hatred that I almost backed up. "It was your fault. Always running around in the middle of the night getting jailed and heaven knows what else . . ." I thought she was going to cuss us out. I really did.

Two-Bit's eyes got narrow and I was afraid he was going to start something. I don't like to hear women get sworn at, even if they deserve it. "No wonder he hates your guts," Two-Bit snapped. He was going to tell her off real good, but I shoved him along. I felt sick. No wonder Johnny didn't want to see her. No wonder he stayed overnight at Two-Bit's or at our house, and slept in the vacant lot in good weather. I remembered my mother . . . beautiful and golden, like Soda, and wise and firm, like Darry.

"Oh, lordy!" There was a catch in Two-Bit's voice and he was closer to tears than I'd ever seen him. "He has to live with that."

We hurried to the elevator to get to the next floor. I hoped the nurse would have enough sense not to let Johnny's mother see him. It would kill him.

Dally was arguing with one of the nurses when we came in. He grinned at us. "Man, am I glad to see you! These ——— hospital people won't let me smoke, and I want out!"

We sat down, grinning at each other. Dally was his usual mean, ornery self. He was okay.

"Shepard came by to see me a while ago."

"That's what Johnny said. What'd he want?"

"Said he saw my picture in the paper and couldn't believe it didn't have 'Wanted Dead or Alive' under it. He mostly came to rub it in about the rumble. Man, I hate not bein' in that."

Only last week Tim Shepard had cracked three of Dally's ribs. But Dally and Tim Shepard had always been buddies; no matter how they fought, they were two of a kind, and they knew it.

Dally was grinning at me. "Kid, you scared the devil outa me the other day. I thought I'd killed you."

"Me?" I said, puzzled. "Why?"

"When you jumped out of the church. I meant to hit you just hard enough to knock you down and put out the fire, but when you dropped like a ton of lead I thought I'd aimed too high and broke your neck." He thought for a minute. "I'm glad I didn't, though."

"I'll bet," I said with a grin. I'd never liked Dally—but then, for the first time, I felt like he was my buddy. And all because he was glad he hadn't killed me.

Dally looked out the window. "Uh . . ."—he sounded very casual—"how's the kid?"

"We just left him," Two-Bit said, and I could tell that he was debating whether to tell Dally the truth or not. "I don't know about stuff like this . . . but . . . well, he seemed pretty bad to me. He passed out cold before we left him."

Dally's jaw line went white as he swore between clenched teeth.

"Two-Bit, you still got that fancy black-handled switch?"

"Yeah."

"Give it here."

Two-Bit reached into his back pocket for his prize possession. It was a jet-handled switchblade, ten inches long, that would flash open at a mere breath. It was the reward of two hours of walking aimlessly around a hardware store to divert suspicion. He kept it razor sharp. As far as I knew, he had never pulled it on anyone; he used his plain pocketknife when he needed a blade. But it was his showpiece, his pride and joy—every time he ran into a new hood he pulled it out and showed off with it. Dally knew how much that knife meant to Two-Bit, and if he needed a blade bad enough to ask for it, well, he needed a blade. That was all there was to it. Two-Bit handed it over to Dally without a moment's hesitation.

"We gotta win that fight tonight," Dally said. His voice was hard. "We gotta get even with the Socs. For Johnny."

He put the switch under his pillow and lay back, staring at the ceiling. We left. We knew better than to talk to Dally when his eyes were blazing and he was in a mood like that.

We decided to catch a bus home. I just didn't feel much

like walking or trying to hitch a ride. Two-Bit left me sitting on the bench at the bus stop while he went to a gas station to buy some cigarettes. I was kind of sick to my stomach and sort of groggy. I was nearly asleep when I felt someone's hand on my forehead. I almost jumped out of my skin. Two-Bit was looking down at me worriedly. "You feel okay? You're awful hot."

"I'm all right," I said, and when he looked at me as if he didn't believe me, I got a little panicky. "Don't tell Darry, okay? Come on, Two-Bit, be a buddy. I'll be well by tonight. I'll take a bunch of aspirins."

"All right," Two-Bit said reluctantly. "But Darry'll kill me if you're really sick and go ahead and fight anyway."

"I'm okay," I said, getting a little angry. "And if you keep your mouth shut, Darry won't know a thing."

"You know somethin'?" Two-Bit said as we were riding home on the bus. "You'd think you could get away with murder, living with your big brother and all, but Darry's stricter with you than your folks were, ain't he?"

"Yeah," I said, "but they'd raised two boys before me. Darry hasn't."

"You know, the only thing that keeps Darry from bein' a Soc is us."

"I know," I said. I had known it for a long time. In spite of not having much money, the only reason Darry couldn't be a Soc was us. The gang. Me and Soda. Darry was too smart to be a greaser. I don't know how I knew, I just did. And I was kind of sorry.

I was silent most of the way home. I was thinking about the rumble. I had a sick feeling in my stomach and it wasn't from being ill. It was the same kind of helplessness I'd felt that night Darry yelled at me for going to sleep in the lot. I had the same deathly fear that something was going to happen that none of us could stop. As we got off the bus I finally said it. "Tonight—I don't like it one bit."

Two-Bit pretended not to understand. "I never knew you to play chicken in a rumble before. Not even when you was a little kid."

I knew he was trying to make me mad, but I took the bait anyway. "I ain't chicken, Two-Bit Mathews, and you know it," I said angrily. "Ain't I a Curtis, same as Soda and Darry?"

Two-Bit couldn't deny this, so I went on: "I mean, I got an awful feeling something's gonna happen."

"Somethin' *is* gonna happen. We're gonna stomp the Socs' guts, that's what."

Two-Bit knew what I meant, but doggedly pretended not to. He seemed to feel that if you said something was all right, it immediately was, no matter what. He's been that way all his life, and I don't expect he'll change. Sodapop would have understood, and we would have tried to figure it out together, but Two-Bit just ain't Soda. Not by a long shot.

Cherry Valance was sitting in her Corvette by the vacant lot when we came by. Her long hair was pinned up, and in daylight she was even better looking. That Sting Ray was one tuff car. A bright red one. It was cool.

"Hi, Ponyboy," she said. "Hi, Two-Bit."

Two-Bit stopped. Apparently Cherry had shown up there before during the week Johnny and I had spent in Windrixville.

"What's up with the big-times?"

She tightened the strings on her ski jacket. "They play your way. No weapons, fair deal. Your rules."

"You sure?"

She nodded. "Randy told me. He knows for sure."

Two-Bit turned and started home. "Thanks, Cherry."

"Ponyboy, stay a minute," Cherry said. I stopped and went back to her car. "Randy's not going to show up at the rumble."

"Yeah," I said, "I know."

"He's not scared. He's just sick of fighting. Bob . . ." She swallowed, then went on quietly. "Bob was his best buddy. Since grade school."

I thought of Soda and Steve. What if one of them saw the other killed? Would that make them stop fighting? No, I thought, maybe it would make Soda stop, but not Steve. He'd go on hating and fighting. Maybe that was what Bob would have done if it had been Randy instead of him.

"How's Johnny?"

"Not so good," I said. "Will you go up to see him?"

She shook her head. "No. I couldn't."

"Why not?" I demanded. It was the least she could do. It was her boyfriend who had caused it all . . . and then I stopped. Her boyfriend . . .

"I couldn't," she said in a quiet, desperate voice. "He killed Bob. Oh, maybe Bob asked for it. I know he did. But I couldn't ever look at the person who killed him. You only knew his bad side. He could be sweet sometimes, and friendly. But when he got drunk . . . it was that part of him that beat up Johnny. I knew it was Bob when you told me the story. He was so proud of his rings. Why do people sell liquor to boys? Why? I know there's a law against it, but kids get it anyway. I can't go see Johnny. I know I'm too young to be in love and all that, but Bob was something special. He wasn't just any boy. He had something that made people follow him, something that marked him different, maybe a little better, than the crowd. Do you know what I mean?"

I did. Cherry saw the same things in Dallas. That was why she was afraid to see him, afraid of loving him. I knew what she meant all right. But she also meant she wouldn't go see Johnny because he had killed Bob. "That's okay," I said sharply. It wasn't Johnny's fault Bob was a booze-hound and Cherry went for boys who were bound for trouble. "I wouldn't want you to see him. You're a traitor to your own kind and not loyal to us. Do you think your spying for us makes up for the fact that you're sitting there in a Corvette while my brother drops out of school to get a job? Don't you ever feel sorry for us. Don't you ever try to give us handouts and then feel high and mighty about it."

I started to turn and walk off, but something in Cherry's face made me stop. I was ashamed—I can't stand to see girls cry. She wasn't crying, but she was close to it.

"I wasn't trying to give you charity, Ponyboy. I only wanted to help. I liked you from the start . . . the way you talked. You're a nice kid, Ponyboy. Do you realize how scarce nice kids are nowadays? Wouldn't you try to help me if you could?"

I would. I'd help her and Randy both, if I could. "Hey," I said suddenly, "can you see the sunset real good from the West Side?"

She blinked, startled, then smiled. "Real good."

"You can see it good from the East Side, too," I said quietly.

"Thanks, Ponyboy." She smiled through her tears. "You dig okay."

She had green eyes. I went on, walking home slowly.

Chapter 9

IT WAS ALMOST SIX-
thirty when I got home. The rumble was set for seven, so I
was late for supper, as usual. I always come in late. I forget
what time it is. Darry had cooked dinner: baked chicken
and potatoes and corn—two chickens because all three of
us eat like horses. Especially Darry. But although I love
baked chicken, I could hardly swallow any. I swallowed
five aspirins, though, when Darry and Soda weren't looking. I do that all the time because I can't sleep very well at
night. Darry thinks I take just one, but I usually take four.
I figured five would keep me going through the rumble
and maybe get rid of my headache.

Then I hurried to take a shower and change clothes.
Me and Soda and Darry always got spruced up before a
rumble. And besides, we wanted to show those Socs we

weren't trash, that we were just as good as they were.

"Soda," I called from the bathroom, "when did you start shaving?"

"When I was fifteen," he yelled back.

"When did Darry?"

"When he was thirteen. Why? You figgerin' on growing a beard for the rumble?"

"You're funny. We ought to send you in to the *Reader's Digest*. I hear they pay a lot for funny things."

Soda laughed and went right on playing poker with Steve in the living room. Darry had on a tight black T-shirt that showed every muscle on his chest and even the flat hard muscles of his stomach. I'd hate to be the Soc who takes a crack at him, I thought as I pulled on a clean T-shirt and a fresh pair of jeans. I wished my T-shirt was tighter—I have a pretty good build for my size, but I'd lost a lot of weight in Windrixville and it just didn't fit right. It was a chilly night and T-shirts aren't the warmest clothes in the world, but nobody ever gets cold in a rumble, and besides, jackets interfere with your swinging ability.

Soda and Steve and I had put on more hair oil than was necessary, but we wanted to show that we were greasers. Tonight we could be proud of it. Greasers may not have much, but they have a rep. That and long hair. (What kind of world is it where all I have to be proud of is a reputation for being a hood, and greasy hair? I don't want to be a hood, but even if I don't steal things and mug people and get boozed up, I'm marked lousy. Why should I be proud of it? Why should I even pretend to be proud of it?) Darry never went in for the long hair. His was short and clean all the time.

I sat in the armchair in the living room, waiting for the rest of the outfit to show up. But of course, tonight the only one coming would be Two-Bit; Johnny and Dallas wouldn't show. Soda and Steve were playing cards and arguing as usual. Soda was keeping up a steady stream of wisecracks and clowning, and Steve had turned up the radio so loud that it almost broke my eardrums. Of course everybody listens to it loud like that, but it wasn't just the best thing for a headache.

"You like fights, don't you, Soda?" I asked suddenly.

"Yeah, sure." He shrugged. "I like fights."

"How come?"

"I don't know." He looked at me, puzzled. "It's action. It's a contest. Like a drag race or a dance or something."

"Shoot," said Steve, "I want to beat those Socs' heads in. When I get in a fight I want to stomp the other guy good. I like it, too."

"How come you like fights, Darry?" I asked, looking up at him as he stood behind me, leaning in the kitchen doorway. He gave me one of those looks that hide what he's thinking, but Soda piped up: "He likes to show off his muscles."

"I'm gonna show 'em off on you, little buddy, if you get any mouthier."

I digested what Soda had said. It was the truth. Darry liked anything that took strength, like weight-lifting or playing football or roofing houses, even if he was proud of being smart too. Darry never said anything about it, but I knew he liked fights. I felt out of things. I'll fight anyone anytime, but I don't like to.

"I don't know if you ought to be in this rumble, Pony," Darry said slowly.

Oh, no, I thought in mortal fear, I've got to be in it. Right then the most important thing in my life was helping us whip the Socs. Don't let him make me stay home now. I've got to be in it.

"How come? I've always come through before, ain't I?"

"Yeah," Darry said with a proud grin. "You fight real good for a kid your size. But you were in shape before. You've lost weight and you don't look so great, kid. You're tensed up too much."

"Shoot," said Soda, trying to get the ace out of his shoe without Steve's seeing him, "we all get tensed up before a rumble. Let him fight tonight. Skin never hurt anyone— no weapons, no danger."

"I'll be okay," I pleaded. "I'll get hold of a little one, okay?"

"Well, Johnny won't be there this time . . ."—Johnny and I sometimes ganged up on one big guy—"but then, Curly Shepard won't be there either, or Dally, and we'll need every man we can get."

"What happened to Shepard?" I asked, remembering Tim Shepard's kid brother. Curly, who was a tough, cool, hard-as-nails Tim in miniature, and I had once played chicken by holding our cigarette ends against each other's fingers. We had stood there, clenching our teeth and grimacing, with sweat pouring down our faces and the smell of burning flesh making us sick, each refusing to holler, until Tim happened to stroll by. When he saw that we were really burning holes in each other he cracked our heads together, swearing to kill us both if we ever pulled a stunt like that again. I still have the scar on my forefinger. Curly was an average downtown hood, tough and not real bright, but I liked him. He could take anything.

"He's in the cooler," Steve said, kicking the ace out of Soda's shoe. "In the reformatory."

Again? I thought, and said, "Let me fight, Darry. If it was blades or chains or something it'd be different. Nobody ever gets really hurt in a skin rumble."

"Well"—Darry gave in—"I guess you can. But be careful, and if you get in a jam, holler and I'll get you out."

"I'll be okay," I said wearily. "How come you never worry about Sodapop as much? I don't see you lecturin' him."

"Man"—Darry grinned and put his arm across Soda's shoulders—"this is one kid brother I don't have to worry about."

Soda punched him in the ribs affectionately.

"This kiddo can use his head."

Sodapop looked down at me with mock superiority, but Darry went on: "You can see he uses it for one thing—to grow hair on." He ducked Soda's swing and took off for the door.

Two-Bit stuck his head in the door just as Darry went flying out of it. Leaping as he went off the steps, Darry turned a somersault in mid-air, hit the ground, and bounced up before Soda could catch him.

"Welup," Two-Bit said cheerfully, cocking an eyebrow, "I see we are in prime condition for a rumble. Is everybody happy?"

"Yeah!" screamed Soda as he too did a flying somersault off the steps. He flipped up to walk on his hands and then did a no-hands cartwheel across the yard to beat Darry's performance. The excitement was catching. Screeching like an Indian, Steve went running across the lawn in flying leaps, stopped suddenly, and flipped backward. We could all do acrobatics because Darry had taken a course at the Y and then spent a whole summer teaching us everything he'd learned on the grounds that it might come in handy in a fight. It did, but it also got Two-Bit and Soda jailed once. They were doing mid-air flips down a downtown sidewalk, walking on their hands, and otherwise disturbing the public and the police. Leave it to those two to pull something like that.

With a happy whoop I did a no-hands cartwheel off the porch steps, hit the ground, and rolled to my feet. Two-Bit followed me in a similar manner.

"I am a greaser," Sodapop chanted. "I am a JD and a hood. I blacken the name of our fair city. I beat up people. I rob gas stations. I am a menace to society. Man, do I have fun!"

"Greaser . . . greaser . . . greaser . . ." Steve singsonged. "O victim of environment, underprivileged, rotten, no-count hood!"

"Juvenile delinquent, you're no good!" Darry shouted.

"Get thee hence, white trash," Two-Bit said in a snobbish voice. "I am a Soc. I am the privileged and the well-dressed. I throw beer blasts, drive fancy cars, break windows at fancy parties."

"And what do you do for fun?" I inquired in a serious, awed voice.

"I jump greasers!" Two-Bit screamed, and did a cartwheel.

We settled down as we walked to the lot. Two-Bit was the only one wearing a jacket; he had a couple of cans of beer stuffed in it. He always gets high before a rumble.

Before anything else, too, come to think of it. I shook my head. I'd hate to see the day when I had to get my nerve from a can. I'd tried drinking once before. The stuff tasted awful, I got sick, had a headache, and when Darry found out, he grounded me for two weeks. But that was the last time I'd ever drink. I'd seen too much of what drinking did for you at Johnny's house.

"Hey, Two-Bit," I said, deciding to complete my survey, "how come you like to fight?"

He looked at me as if I was off my nut. "Shoot, everybody fights."

If everybody jumped in the Arkansas River, ol' Two-Bit would be right on their heels. I had it then(Soda fought for fun, Steve for hatred, Darry for pride, and Two-Bit for conformity. Why do I fight? I thought, and couldn't think of any real good reason. There isn't any real good reason for fighting except self-defense.)

"Listen, Soda, you and Ponyboy," Darry said as we strode down the street, "if the fuzz show, you two beat it out of there. The rest of us can only get jailed. You two can get sent to a boys' home."

"Nobody in this neighborhood's going to call the fuzz," Steve said grimly. "They know what'd happen if they did."

"All the same, you two blow at the first sign of trouble. You hear me?"

"You sure don't need an amplifier," Soda said, and stuck out his tongue at the back of Darry's head. I stifled a giggle. If you want to see something funny, it's a tough hood sticking his tongue out at his big brother.

———————

Tim Shepard and company were already waiting when we
arrived at the vacant lot, along with a gang from Brumly,
one of the suburbs. Tim was a lean, catlike eighteen-year-
old who looked like the model JD you see in movies and
magazines. He had the right curly black hair, smoldering
dark eyes, and a long scar from temple to chin where a
tramp had belted him with a broken pop bottle. He had a
tough, hard look to him, and his nose had been broken
twice. Like Dally's, his smile was grim and bitter. He was
one of those who enjoy being a hood. The rest of his
bunch were the same way. The boys from Brumly, too.
Young hoods—who would grow up to be old hoods. I'd
never thought about it before, but they'd just get worse as
they got older, not better. I looked at Darry. He wasn't
going to be any hood when he got old. He was going to get
somewhere. Living the way we do would only make him
more determined to get somewhere. That's why he's better
than the rest of us, I thought. He's going somewhere. And
I was going to be like him. I wasn't going to live in a lousy
neighborhood all my life.

Tim had the tense, hungry look of an alley cat—that's
what he's always reminded me of, an alley cat—and he was
constantly restless. His boys ranged from fifteen to nine-
teen, hard-looking characters who were used to the strict
discipline Tim gave out. That was the difference between
his gang and ours—they had a leader and were organized;
we were just buddies who stuck together—each man was
his own leader. Maybe that was why we could whip them.

Tim and the leader of the Brumly outfit moved forward
to shake hands with each of us—proving that our gangs
were on the same side in this fight, although most of the

guys in those two outfits weren't exactly what I'd like to call my friends. When Tim got to me he studied me, maybe remembering how his kid brother and I had played chicken. "You and the quiet black-headed kid were the ones who killed that Soc?"

"Yeah," I said, pretending to be proud of it; then I thought of Cherry and Randy and got a sick feeling in my stomach.

"Good goin', kid. Curly always said you were a good kid. Curly's in the reformatory for the next six months." Tim grinned ruefully, probably thinking of his roughneck, hard-headed brother. "He got caught breakin' into a liquor store, the little . . ." He went on to call Curly every unprintable name under the sun—in Tim's way of thinking, terms of affection.

I surveyed the scene with pride. I was the youngest one there. Even Curly, if he had been there, had turned fifteen, so he was older than me. I could tell Darry realized this too, and although he was proud, I also knew he was worried. Shoot, I thought, I'll fight so good this time he won't ever worry about me again. I'll show him that someone besides Sodapop can use his head.

One of the Brumly guys waved me over. We mostly stuck with our own outfits, so I was a little leery of going over to him, but I shrugged. He asked to borrow a weed, then lit up. "That big guy with y'all, you know him pretty well?"

"I ought to, he's my brother," I said. I couldn't honestly say "Yes." I knew Darry as well as he knew me, and that isn't saying a whole lot.

"No kiddin'? I got a feelin' he's gonna be asked to start

the fireworks around here. He a pretty good bopper?"

He meant rumbler. Those Brumly boys have weird vocabularies. I doubt if half of them can read a newspaper or spell much more than their names, and it comes out in their speech. I mean, you take a guy that calls a rumble "bop-action," and you can tell he isn't real educated.

"Yep," I said. "But why him?"

He shrugged. "Why anybody else?"

I looked our outfits over. Most greasers don't have real tuff builds or anything. They're mostly lean and kind of panther-looking in a slouchy way. This is partly because they don't eat much and partly because they're slouchy. Darry looked like he could whip anyone there. I think most of the guys were nervous because of the 'no weapons' rule. I didn't know about the Brumly boys, but I knew Shepard's gang were used to fighting with anything they could get their hands on—bicycle chains, blades, pop bottles, pieces of pipe, pool sticks, or sometimes even heaters. I mean guns. I have a kind of lousy vocabulary, too, even if I am educated. Our gang never went in for weapons. We're just not that rough. The only weapons we ever used were knives, and shoot, we carried them mostly just for looks. Like Two-Bit with his black-handled switch. None of us had ever really hurt anybody, or wanted to. Just Johnny. And he hadn't wanted to.

"Hey, Curtis!" Tim yelled. I jumped.

"Which one?" I heard Soda yell back.

"The big one. Come on over here."

The guy from Brumly looked at me. "What did I tell ya?"

I watched Darry going toward Tim and the leader of the Brumly boys. He shouldn't be here, I thought suddenly. I shouldn't be here and Steve shouldn't be here and Soda shouldn't be here and Two-Bit shouldn't be here. We're greasers, but not hoods, and we don't belong with this bunch of future convicts. We could end up like them, I thought. We could. And the thought didn't help my headache.

I went back to stand with Soda and Steve and Two-Bit then, because the Socs were arriving. Right on time. They came in four carloads, and filed out silently. I counted twenty-two of them. There were twenty of us, so I figured the odds were as even as we could get them. Darry always liked to take on two at a time anyway. They looked like they were all cut from the same piece of cloth: clean-shaven with semi-Beatle haircuts, wearing striped or checkered shirts with light-red or tan-colored jackets or madras ski jackets. They could just as easily have been going to the movies as to a rumble. That's why people don't ever think to blame the Socs and are always ready to jump on us. We look hoody and they look decent. It could be just the other way around—half of the hoods I know are pretty decent guys underneath all that grease, and from what I've heard, a lot of Socs are just cold-blooded mean— but people usually go by looks.

They lined up silently, facing us, and we lined up facing them. I looked for Randy but didn't see him. I hoped he wasn't there. A guy with a madras shirt stepped up. "Let's get the rules straight—nothing but our fists, and the first to run lose. Right?"

Tim flipped away his beer can. "You savvy real good."

There was an uneasy silence: Who was going to start it? Darry solved the problem. He stepped forward under the circle of light made by the street lamp. For a minute, everything looked unreal, like a scene out of a JD movie or something. Then Darry said, "I'll take on anyone."

He stood there, tall, broad-shouldered, his muscles taut under his T-shirt and his eyes glittering like ice. For a second it looked like there wasn't anyone brave enough to take him on. Then there was a slight stir in the faceless mob of Socs, and a husky blond guy stepped forward. He looked at Darry and said quietly, "Hello, Darrel."

Something flickered behind Darry's eyes and then they were ice again. "Hello, Paul."

I heard Soda give a kind of squeak and I realized that the blond was Paul Holden. He had been the best halfback on Darry's football team at high school and he and Darry used to buddy it around all the time. He must be a junior in college by now, I thought. He was looking at Darry with an expression I couldn't quite place, but disliked. Contempt? Pity? Hate? All three? Why? Because Darry was standing there representing all of us, and maybe Paul felt only contempt and pity and hate for greasers? Darry hadn't moved a muscle or changed expression, but you could see he hated Paul now. It wasn't only jealousy— Darry had a right to be jealous; he was ashamed to be on our side, ashamed to be seen with the Brumly boys, Shepard's gang, maybe even us. Nobody realized it but me and Soda. It didn't matter to anyone but me and Soda.

That's stupid, I thought swiftly, they've both come here to fight and they're both supposed to be smarter than that. What difference does the side make?

Then Paul said, "I'll take you," and something like a smile crossed Darry's face. I knew Darry had thought he could take Paul any time. But that was two or three years ago. What if Paul was better now? I swallowed. Neither one of my brothers had ever been beaten in a fight, but I wasn't exactly itching for someone to break the record.

They moved in a circle under the light, counterclockwise, eyeing each other, sizing each other up, maybe remembering old faults and wondering if they were still there. The rest of us waited with mounting tension. I was reminded of Jack London's books—you know, where the wolf pack waits in silence for one of two members to go down in a fight. But it was different here. The moment either one swung a punch, the rumble would be on.

The silence grew heavier, and I could hear the harsh heavy breathing of the boys around me. Still Darry and the Soc walked slowly in a circle. Even I could feel their hatred. They used to be buddies, I thought, they used to be friends, and now they hate each other because one has to work for a living and the other comes from the West Side. They shouldn't hate each other . . . I don't hate the Socs any more . . . they shouldn't hate . . .

"Hold up!" a familiar voice yelled. "Hold it!" Darry turned to see who it was, and Paul swung—a hard right to the jaw that would have felled anyone but Darry. The rumble was on. Dallas Winston ran to join us.

I couldn't find a Soc my size, so I took the next-best size and jumped on him. Dallas was right beside me, already on top of someone.

"I thought you were in the hospital," I yelled as the Soc knocked me to the ground and I rolled to avoid getting kicked.

"I was." Dally was having a hard time because his left

arm was still in bad shape. "I ain't now."

"How?" I managed to ask as the Soc I was fighting leaped on me and we rolled near Dally.

"Talked the nurse into it with Two-Bit's switch. Don't you know a rumble ain't a rumble unless I'm in it?"

I couldn't answer because the Soc, who was heavier than I took him for, had me pinned and was slugging the sense out of me. I thought dizzily that he was going to knock some of my teeth loose or break my nose or something, and I knew I didn't have a chance. But Darry was keeping an eye out for me; he caught that guy by the shoulder and half lifted him up before knocking him three feet with a sledge-hammer blow. I decided it would be fair for me to help Dally since he could use only one arm.

They were slugging it out, but Dallas was getting the worst of it, so I jumped on his Soc's back, pulling his hair and pounding him. He reached back and caught me by the neck and threw me over his head to the ground. Tim Shepard, who was fighting two at once, accidentally stepped on me, knocking my breath out. I was up again as soon as I got my wind, and jumped right back on the Soc, trying my best to strangle him. While he was prying my fingers loose, Dally knocked him backward, so that all three of us rolled on the ground, gasping, cussing, and punching.

Somebody kicked me hard in the ribs and I yelped in spite of myself. Some Soc had knocked out one of our bunch and was kicking me as hard as he could. But I had both arms wrapped around the other Soc's neck and refused to let go. Dally was slugging him, and I hung on desperately, although that other Soc was kicking me and you'd better believe it hurt. Finally he kicked me in the head so hard it stunned me, and I lay limp, trying to clear my mind and keep from blacking out. I could hear the racket, but only dimly through the buzzing in my ears. Numerous bruises along my back and on my face were throbbing, but I felt detached from the pain, as if it wasn't really me feeling it.

"They're running!" I heard a voice yell joyfully. "Look at the dirty —— run!"

It seemed to me that the voice belonged to Two-Bit, but I couldn't be sure. I tried to sit up, and saw that the Socs were getting into their cars and leaving. Tim Shepard was swearing blue and green because his nose was broken again, and the leader of the Brumly boys was working over one of his own men because he had broken the rules and used a piece of pipe in the fighting. Steve lay doubled up and groaning about ten feet from me. We found out later he had three broken ribs. Sodapop was beside him, talking in a low steady voice. I did a double take when I saw Two-Bit—blood was streaming down one side of his face and one hand was busted wide open; but he was grinning happily because the Socs were running.

"We won," Darry announced in a tired voice. He was going to have a black eye and there was a cut across his forehead. "We beat the Socs."

Dally stood beside me quietly for a minute, trying to grasp the fact that we had really beaten the Socs. Then, grabbing my shirt, he hauled me to my feet. "Come on!" He half dragged me down the street. "We're goin' to see Johnny."

I tried to run but stumbled, and Dally impatiently

shoved me along. "Hurry! He was gettin' worse when I left. He wants to see you."

I don't know how Dallas could travel so fast and hard after being knocked around and having his sore arm hurt some more, but I tried to keep up with him. Track wasn't ever like the running I did that night. I was still dizzy and had only a dim realization of where I was going and why.

Dally had Buck Merril's T-bird parked in front of our house, and we hopped into it. I sat tight as Dally roared the car down the street. We were on Tenth when a siren came on behind us and I saw the reflection of the red light flashing in the windshield.

"Look sick," Dally commanded. "I'll say I'm taking you to the hospital, which'll be truth enough."

I leaned against the cold glass of the window and tried to look sick, which wasn't too hard, feeling the way I did right then.

The policeman looked disgusted. "All right, buddy, where's the fire?"

"The kid"—Dally jerked a thumb toward me—"he fell over on his motorcycle and I'm takin' him to the hospital."

I groaned, and it wasn't all fake-out. I guess I looked pretty bad, too, being cut and bruised like I was.

The fuzz changed his tone. "Is he real bad? Do you need an escort?"

"How would I know if he's bad or not? I ain't no doc. Yeah, we could use an escort." And as the policeman got back into his car I heard Dally hiss, "Sucker!"

With the siren ahead of us, we made record time getting to the hospital. All the way there Dally kept talking and talking about something, but I was too dizzy to make most of it out.

"I was crazy, you know that, kid? Crazy for wantin' Johnny to stay outa trouble, for not wantin' him to get hard. If he'd been like me he'd never have been in this mess. If he'd got smart like me he'd never have run into that church. That's what you get for helpin' people. Editorials in the paper and a lot of trouble. . . . You'd better wise up, Pony . . . you get tough like me and you don't get hurt. You look out for yourself and nothin' can touch you . . ."

He said a lot more stuff, but I didn't get it all. I had a stupid feeling that Dally was out of his mind, the way he kept raving on and on, because Dallas never talked like that, but I think now I would have understood if I hadn't been sick at the time.

The cop left us at the hospital as Dally pretended to help me out of the car. The minute the cop was gone, Dally let go of me so quick I almost fell. "Hurry!"

We ran through the lobby and crowded past people into the elevator. Several people yelled at us, I think because we were pretty racked-up looking, but Dally had nothing on his mind except Johnny, and I was too mixed up to know anything but that I had to follow Dally. When we finally got to Johnny's room, the doctor stopped us. "I'm sorry, boys, but he's dying."

"We gotta see him," Dally said, and flicked out Two-Bit's switchblade. His voice was shaking. "We're gonna see him and if you give me any static you'll end up on your own operatin' table."

The doctor didn't bat an eye. "You can see him, but it's because you're his friends, not because of that knife."

Dally looked at him for a second, then put the knife back in his pocket. We both went into Johnny's room, standing there for a second, getting our breath back in heavy gulps. It was awful quiet. It was scary quiet. I looked at Johnny. He was very still, and for a moment I thought in agony: He's dead already. We're too late.

Dally swallowed, wiping the sweat off his upper lip. "Johnnycake?" he said in a hoarse voice. "Johnny?"

Johnny stirred weakly, then opened his eyes. "Hey," he managed softly.

"We won," Dally panted. "We beat the Socs. We stomped them—chased them outa our territory."

Johnny didn't even try to grin at him. "Useless . . . fighting's no good. . . ." He was awful white.

Dally licked his lips nervously. "They're still writing editorials about you in the paper. For being a hero and all." He was talking too fast and too calmly. "Yeah, they're calling you a hero now and heroizin' all the greasers. We're all proud of you, buddy."

Johnny's eyes glowed. Dally was proud of him. That was all Johnny had ever wanted.

"Ponyboy."

I barely heard him. I came closer and leaned over to hear what he was going to say.

"Stay gold, Ponyboy. Stay gold . . ." The pillow seemed to sink a little, and Johnny died.

You read about people looking peacefully asleep when they're dead, but they don't. Johnny just looked dead. Like a candle with the flame gone. I tried to say something, but I couldn't make a sound.

Dally swallowed and reached over to push Johnny's hair back. "Never could keep that hair back . . . that's what you get for tryin' to help people, you little punk, that's what you get . . ."

Whirling suddenly, he slammed back against the wall. His face contracted in agony, and sweat streamed down his face.

"Damnit, Johnny . . ." he begged, slamming one fist against the wall, hammering it to make it obey his will. "Oh, damnit, Johnny, don't die, please don't die . . ."

He suddenly bolted through the door and down the hall.

Chapter 10

I WALKED DOWN THE
hall in a daze. Dally had taken the car and I started
the long walk home in a stupor. Johnny was dead. But he
wasn't. That still body back in the hospital wasn't Johnny.
Johnny was somewhere else—maybe asleep in the lot, or
playing the pinball machine in the bowling alley, or sitting
on the back steps of the church in Windrixville. I'd go
home and walk by the lot, and Johnny would be sitting on
the curb smoking a cigarette, and maybe we'd lie on our
backs and watch the stars. He isn't dead, I said to myself.
He isn't dead. And this time my dreaming worked. I convinced myself that he wasn't dead.

I must have wandered around for hours; sometimes
even out into the street, getting honked at and cussed out.

I might have stumbled around all night except for a man who asked me if I wanted a ride.

"Huh? Oh. Yeah, I guess so," I said. I got in. The man, who was in his mid-twenties, looked at me.

"Are you all right, kid? You look like you've been in a fight."

"I have been. A rumble. I'm okay." Johnny is *not* dead, I told myself, and I believed it.

"Hate to tell you this, kiddo," the guy said dryly, "but you're bleedin' all over my car seats."

I blinked. "I am?"

"Your head."

I reached up to scratch the side of my head where it'd been itching for a while, and when I looked at my hand it was smeared with blood.

"Gosh, mister, I'm sorry," I said, dumfounded.

"Don't worry about it. This wreck's been through worse. What's your address? I'm not about to dump a hurt kid out on the streets this time of night."

I told him. He drove me to my house, and I got out. "Thanks a lot."

What was left of our gang was in the living room. Steve was stretched out on the sofa, his shirt unbuttoned and his side bandaged. His eyes were closed, but when the door shut behind me he opened them, and I suddenly wondered if my own eyes looked as feverish and bewildered as his. Soda had a wide cut on his lip and a bruise across his cheek. There was a Band-Aid over Darry's forehead and he had a black eye. One side of Two-Bit's face was taped up— I found out later he had four stitches in his cheek and seven in his hand where he had busted his knuckles open over a Soc's head. They were lounging around, reading the paper and smoking.

Where's the party? I thought dully. Weren't Soda and Steve planning a party after the rumble? They all looked up when I walked in. Darry leaped to his feet.

"Where have you been?"

Oh, let's don't start that again, I thought. He stopped suddenly.

"Ponyboy, what's the matter?"

I looked at all of them, a little frightened. "Johnny . . . he's dead." My voice sounded strange, even to me. But he's not dead, a voice in my head said. "We told him about beatin' the Socs and . . . I don't know, he just died." He told me to stay gold, I remembered. What was he talking about?

There was a stricken silence. I don't think any of us had realized how bad off Johnny really had been. Soda made a funny noise and looked like he was going to start crying. Two-Bit's eyes were closed and his teeth were clenched, and I suddenly remembered Dally. . . . Dally pounding on the wall . . .

"Dallas is gone," I said. "He ran out like the devil was after him. He's gonna blow up. He couldn't take it."

How can I take it? I wondered. Dally is tougher than I am. Why can I take it when Dally can't? And then I knew. Johnny was the only thing Dally loved. And now Johnny was gone.

"So he finally broke." Two-Bit spoke everyone's feelings. "So even Dally has a breaking point."

I started shaking. Darry said something in a low voice to Soda.

"Ponyboy," Soda said softly, like he was talking to an injured animal, "you look sick. Sit down."

I backed up, just like a frightened animal, shaking my head. "I'm okay." I felt sick. I felt as if any minute I was going to fall flat on my face, but I shook my head. "I don't want to sit down."

Darry took a step toward me, but I backed away. "Don't touch me," I said. My heart was pounding in slow thumps, throbbing at the side of my head, and I wondered if everyone else could hear it. Maybe that's why they're all looking at me, I thought, they can hear my heart beating . . .

The phone rang, and after a moment's hesitation, Darry turned from me to it. He said "Hello" and then listened. He hung up quickly.

"It was Dally. He phoned from a booth. He's just robbed a grocery store and the cops are after him. We gotta hide him. He'll be at the lot in a minute."

We all left the house at a dead run, even Steve, and I wondered vaguely why no one was doing somersaults off the steps this time. Things were sliding in and out of focus, and it seemed funny to me that I couldn't run in a straight line.

We reached the vacant lot just as Dally came in, running as hard as he could, from the opposite direction. The wail of a siren grew louder and then a police car pulled up across the street from the lot. Doors slammed as the policemen leaped out. Dally had reached the circle of light under the street lamp, and skidding to a halt, he turned and jerked a black object from his waistband. I remembered his voice: *I been carryin' a heater. It ain't loaded, but it sure does help a bluff.*

It was only yesterday that Dally had told Johnny and me that. But yesterday was years ago. A lifetime ago.

Dally raised the gun, and I thought: You blasted fool. They don't know you're only bluffing. And even as the policemen's guns spit fire into the night I knew that was what Dally wanted. He was jerked half around by the impact of the bullets, then slowly crumpled with a look of grim triumph on his face. He was dead before he hit the ground. But I knew that was what he wanted, even as the lot echoed with the cracks of shots, even as I begged silently—Please, not him . . . not him and Johnny both—I knew he would be dead, because Dally Winston wanted to be dead and he always got what he wanted.

Nobody would write editorials praising Dally. Two friends of mine had died that night: one a hero, the other a hoodlum. But I remembered Dally pulling Johnny through the window of the burning church; Dally giving us his gun, although it could mean jail for him; Dally risking his life for us, trying to keep Johnny out of trouble. And now he was a dead juvenile delinquent and there wouldn't be any editorials in his favor. Dally didn't die a hero. He died violent and young and desperate, just like we all knew he'd die someday. Just like Tim Shepard and Curly Shepard and the Brumly boys and the other guys we knew would die someday. But Johnny was right. He died gallant.

Steve stumbled forward with a sob, but Soda caught him by the shoulders.

"Easy, buddy, easy," I heard him say softly, "there's nothing we can do now."

Nothing we can do . . . not for Dally or Johnny or Tim Shepard or any of us . . . My stomach gave a violent start and turned into a hunk of ice. The world was spinning around me, and blobs of faces and visions of things past were dancing in the red mist that covered the lot. It swirled into a mass of colors and I felt myself swaying on my feet. Someone cried, "Glory, look at the kid!"

And the ground rushed up to meet me very suddenly.

When I woke up it was light. It was awfully quiet. Too quiet. I mean, our house just isn't naturally quiet. The radio's usually going full blast and the TV is turned up loud and people are wrestling and knocking over lamps and tripping over the coffee table and yelling at each other. Something was wrong, but I couldn't quite figure it out. Something had happened . . . I couldn't remember what. I blinked at Soda bewilderedly. He was sitting on the edge of the bed watching me.

"Soda . . ."—my voice sounded weak and hoarse—"is somebody sick?"

"Yeah." His voice was oddly gentle. "Go back to sleep now."

An idea was slowly dawning on me. "Am *I* sick?"

He stroked my hair. "Yeah, you're sick. Now be quiet."

I had one more question. I was still kind of mixed up. "Is Darry sorry I'm sick?" I had a funny feeling that Darry was sad because I was sick. Everything seemed vague and hazy.

Soda gave me a funny look. He was quiet for a moment. "Yeah, he's sorry you're sick. Now please shut up, will ya, honey? Go back to sleep."

I closed my eyes. I was awful tired.

When I woke up next, it was daylight and I was hot under all the blankets on me. I was thirsty and hungry, but my stomach was so uneasy I knew I wouldn't be able to hold anything down. Darry had pulled the armchair into the bedroom and was asleep in it. He should be at work, I thought. Why is he asleep in the armchair?

"Hey, Darry," I said softly, shaking his knee. "Hey, Darry, wake up."

He opened his eyes. "Ponyboy, you okay?"

"Yeah," I said, "I think so."

Something had happened . . . but I still couldn't remember it, although I was thinking a lot clearer than I was the last time I'd waked up.

He sighed in relief and pushed my hair back. "Gosh, kid, you had us scared to death."

"What was the matter with me?"

He shook his head. "I told you you were in no condition for a rumble. Exhaustion, shock, minor concussion—and Two-Bit came blubberin' over here with some tale about how you were running a fever before the rumble and how it was all his fault you were sick. He was pretty torn up that night," Darry said. He was quiet for a minute. "We all were."

And then I remembered. Dallas and Johnny were dead. Don't think of them, I thought. (Don't remember how Johnny was your buddy, don't remember that he didn't want to die. Don't think of Dally breaking up in the hospital, crumpling under the street light. Try to think that Johnny is better off now, try to remember that Dally would have ended up like that sooner or later. Best of all, don't think. Blank your mind. Don't remember. Don't remember.)

"Where'd I get a concussion?" I said. My head itched, but I couldn't scratch it for the bandage. "How long have I been asleep?"

"You got a concussion from getting kicked in the head— Soda saw it. He landed all over that Soc. I've never seen him so mad. I think he could have whipped anyone, in the state he was in. Today's Tuesday, and you've been asleep and delirious since Saturday night. Don't you remember?"

"No," I said slowly. "Darry, I'm not ever going to be able to make up the school I've missed. And I've still got to go to court and talk to the police about Bob's getting killed. And now . . . with Dally . . ."—I took a deep breath—"Darry, do you think they'll split us up? Put me in a home or something?"

He was silent. "I don't know, baby. I just don't know."

I stared at the ceiling. What would it be like, I wondered, staring at a different ceiling? What would it be like in a different bed, in a different room? There was a hard painful lump in my throat that I couldn't swallow.

"Don't you even remember being in the hospital?" Darry asked. He was trying to change the subject.

I shook my head. "I don't remember."

"You kept asking for me and Soda. Sometimes for Mom and Dad, too. But mostly for Soda."

Something in his tone of voice made me look at him. Mostly for Soda. Did I ask for Darry at all, or was he just saying that?

"Darry . . ." I didn't know quite what I wanted to say. But I had a sick feeling that maybe I hadn't called for him while I was delirious, maybe I had only wanted Sodapop to be with me. What all had I said while I was sick? I couldn't remember. I didn't want to remember.

"Johnny left you his copy of *Gone with the Wind*. Told the nurse he wanted you to have it."

I looked at the paperback lying on the table. I didn't want to finish it. I'd never get past the part where the Southern gentlemen go riding into sure death because they are gallant. Southern gentlemen with big black eyes in blue jeans and T-shirts, Southern gentlemen crumpling under street lights. Don't remember. Don't try to decide which one died gallant. Don't remember.

"Where's Soda?" I asked, and then I could have kicked myself. Why can't you talk to Darry, you idiot? I said to myself. Why do you feel uncomfortable talking to Darry?

"Asleep, I hope. I thought he was going to go to sleep shaving this morning and cut his throat. I had to push him to bed, but he was out like a light in a second."

Darry's hopes that Soda was asleep were immediately ruined, because he came running in, clad only in a pair of blue jeans.

"Hey, Ponyboy!" he yelped, and leaped for me, but Darry caught him.

"No rough stuff, little buddy."

So Soda had to content himself with bouncing up and down on the bed and pounding on my shoulder.

"Gosh, but you were sick. You feel okay now?"

"I'm okay. Just a little hungry."

"I should think you would be," Darry said. "You wouldn't eat anything most of the time you were sick. How'd you like some mushroom soup?"

I suddenly realized just how empty I was. "Man, I'd like that just fine."

"I'll go make some. Sodapop, take it easy with him, okay?"

Soda looked back at him indignantly. "You'd think I was going to challenge him to a track meet or something right off the bat."

"Oh, no," I groaned. "Track meet. I guess this just about puts me out of every race. I won't be back in condition for the meets. And the coach was counting on me."

"Golly, there's always next year," Soda said. Soda never has grasped the importance Darry and I put on athletics. Like he never has understood why we went all-out for studying. "Don't sweat it about some track meet."

"Soda," I said suddenly. "What all did I say while I was delirious?"

"Oh, you thought you were in Windrixville most of the time. Then you kept saying that Johnny didn't mean to kill that Soc. Hey, I didn't know you didn't like baloney."

I went cold. "I don't like it. I never liked it."

Soda just looked at me. "You used to eat it. That's why you wouldn't eat anything while you were sick. You kept saying you didn't like baloney, no matter what it was we were trying to get you to eat."

"I don't like it," I repeated. "Soda, did I ask for Darry while I was sick?"

"Yeah, sure," he said, looking at me strangely. "You asked for him and me both. Sometimes Mom and Dad. And for Johnny."

"Oh. I thought maybe I didn't ask for Darry. It was bugging me."

Soda grinned. "Well, you did, so don't worry. We stayed with you so much that the doctor told us we were going to end up in the hospital ourselves if we didn't get some sleep. But we didn't get any anyway."

I took a good look at him. He looked completely worn out; there were circles under his eyes and he had a tense, tired look to him. Yet his dark eyes were still laughing and carefree and reckless.

"You look beat," I said frankly. "I bet you ain't had three hours sleep since Saturday night."

He grinned but didn't deny it. "Scoot over." He crawled over me and flopped down and before Darry came back in with the soup we were both asleep.

Chapter 11

I HAD TO STAY IN BED a whole week after that. That bugged me; I'm not the kind that can lie around looking at the ceiling all the time. I read most of the time, and drew pictures. One day I started flipping through one of Soda's old yearbooks and came across a picture that seemed vaguely familiar. Not even when I read the name Robert Sheldon did it hit me who it was. And then I finally realized it was Bob. I took a real good long look at it.

The picture didn't look a whole lot like the Bob I remembered, but nobody ever looks a whole lot like his picture in a yearbook anyway. He had been a sophomore that year—that would make him about eighteen when he died. Yeah, he was good-looking even then, with a grin that reminded me of Soda's, a kind of reckless grin. He had

been a handsome black-haired boy with dark eyes—maybe
brown, like Soda's, maybe dark-blue, like the Shepard
boys'. Maybe he'd had black eyes. Like Johnny. I had
never given Bob much thought—I hadn't had time to
think. But that day I wondered about him. What was
he like?

I knew he liked to pick fights, had the usual Soc belief
that living on the West Side made you Mr. Super-Tuff,
looked good in dark wine-colored sweaters, and was proud
of his rings. But what about the Bob Sheldon that Cherry
Valance knew? She was a smart girl; she didn't like him
just because he was good-looking. Sweet and friendly,
stands out from the crowd—that's what she had said. A real
person, the best buddy a guy ever had, kept trying to make
somebody stop him—Randy had told me that. Did he
have a kid brother who idolized him? Maybe a big brother
who kept bugging him not to be so wild? His parents let
him run wild—because they loved him too much or too
little? Did they hate us now? I hoped they hated us, that
they weren't full of that pity-the-victims-of-environment
junk the social workers kept handing Curly Shepard every
time he got sent off to reform school. I'd rather have anybody's hate than their pity. But, then, maybe they understood, like Cherry Valance. I looked at Bob's picture and I
could begin to see the person we had killed. A reckless,
hot-tempered boy, cocky and scared stiff at the same time.

"Ponyboy."

"Yeah?" I didn't look up. I thought it was the doctor.
He'd been coming over to see me almost every day,
although he didn't do much except talk to me.

"There's a guy here to see you. Says he knows you."
Something in Darry's voice made me look up, and his eyes
were hard. "His name's Randy."

"Yeah, I know him," I said.

"You want to see him?"

"Yeah." I shrugged. "Sure, why not?"

A few guys from school had dropped by to see me; I
have quite a few friends at school even if I am younger
than most of them and don't talk much. But that's what
they are—school friends, not buddies. I had been glad to
see them, but it bothered me because we live in kind of a
lousy neighborhood and our house isn't real great. It's run-
down looking and everything, and the inside's kind of
poor-looking, too, even though for a bunch of boys we do a
pretty good job of house-cleaning. Most of my friends at
school come from good homes, not filthy-rich like the
Socs, but middle-class, anyway. It was a funny thing—it
bugged me about my friends seeing our house. But I
couldn't have cared less about what Randy thought.

"Hi, Ponyboy." Randy looked uncomfortable standing
in the doorway.

"Hi, Randy," I said. "Have a seat if you can find one."
Books were lying all over everything. He pushed a couple
off a chair and sat down.

"How you feeling? Cherry told me your name was on
the school bulletin."

"I'm okay. You can't really miss my name on any kind of
bulletin."

He still looked uncomfortable, although he tried to grin.

"Wanna smoke?" I offered him a weed, but he shook

his head. "No, thanks. Uh, Ponyboy, one reason I came here was to see if you were okay, but you—we—got to go see the judge tomorrow."

"Yeah," I said, lighting a cigarette. "I know. Hey, holler if you see one of my brothers coming. I'll catch it for smoking in bed."

"My dad says for me to tell the truth and nobody can get hurt. He's kind of upset about all this. I mean, my dad's a good guy and everything, better than most, and I kind of let him down, being mixed up in all this."

I just looked at him. That was the dumbest remark I ever heard anyone make. He thought *he* was mixed up in this? He didn't kill anyone, he didn't get his head busted in a rumble, it wasn't his buddy that was shot down under a street light. Besides, what did he have to lose? His old man was rich, he could pay whatever fine there was for being drunk and picking a fight.

"I wouldn't mind getting fined," Randy said, "but I feel lousy about the old man. And it's the first time I've felt anything in a long time."

The only thing I'd felt in a long time was being scared. Scared stiff. I'd put off thinking about the judge and the hearing for as long as I could. Soda and Darry didn't like to talk about it either, so we were all silently counting off the days while I was sick, counting the days that we had left together. But with Randy sticking solidly to the subject it was impossible to think about anything else. My cigarette started trembling.

"I guess your folks feel kind of awful about it, too."

"My parents are dead. I live here with just Darry and Soda, my brothers." I took a long drag on my cigarette.

"That's what's worrying me. If the judge decides Darry isn't a good guardian or something, I'm liable to get stuck in a home somewhere. That's the rotten part of this deal. Darry *is* a good guardian; he makes me study and knows where I am and who I'm with all the time. I mean, we don't get along so great sometimes, but he keeps me out of trouble, or did. My father didn't yell at me as much as he does."

"I didn't know that." Randy looked worried, he really did. A Soc, even, worried because some kid greaser was on his way to a foster home or something. That was really funny. I don't mean funny. You know what I mean.

"Listen to me, Pony. You didn't do anything. It was your friend Johnny that had the knife . . ."

"I had it." I stopped him. He was looking at me strangely. "I had the knife. I killed Bob."

Randy shook his head. "I saw it. You were almost drowned. It was the black-headed guy that had the switchblade. Bob scared him into doing it. I saw it."

I was bewildered. "I killed him. I had a switchblade and I was scared they were going to beat me up."

"No, kid, it was your friend, the one who died in the hospital . . ."

"Johnny is not dead." My voice was shaking. "Johnny is not dead."

"Hey, Randy." Darry stuck his head in the door. "I think you'd better go now."

"Sure," Randy said. He was still looking at me kind of funny. "See you around, Pony."

"Don't ever say anything to him about Johnny," I heard Darry say in a low voice as they went out. "He's still pretty racked up mentally and emotionally. The doc said he'd get over it if we gave him time."

I swallowed hard and blinked. He was just like all the rest of the Socs. Cold-blooded mean. Johnny didn't have anything to do with Bob's getting killed.

"Ponyboy Curtis, put out that cigarette!"

"Okay, okay." I put it out. "I ain't going to go to sleep smoking, Darry. If you make me stay in bed there ain't anywhere else I can smoke."

"You're not going to die if you don't get a smoke. But if that bed catches on fire you will. You couldn't make it to the door through that mess."

"Well, golly, I can't pick it up and Soda doesn't, so I guess that leaves you."

He was giving me one of those looks. "All right, all right," I said, "that don't leave you. Maybe Soda'll straighten it up a little."

"Maybe you can be a little neater, huh, little buddy?"

He'd never called me that before. Soda was the only one he ever called "little buddy."

"Sure," I said, "I'll be more careful."

Chapter 12

THE HEARING WASN'T anything like I thought it would be. Besides Darry and Soda and me, nobody was there except Randy and his parents and Cherry Valance and her parents and a couple of the other guys that had jumped Johnny and me that night. I don't know what I expected the whole thing to be like—I guess I've been watching too many Perry Mason shows. Oh, yeah, the doctor was there and he had a long talk with the judge before the hearing. I didn't know what he had to do with it then, but I do now.

First Randy was questioned. He looked a little nervous, and I wished they'd let him have a cigarette. I wished they'd let *me* have a cigarette; I was more than a little shaky myself. Darry had told me to keep my mouth shut no matter what Randy and everybody said, that I'd get my turn.

All the Socs told the same story and stuck mainly to the truth, except they said Johnny had killed Bob; but I figured I could straighten that point out when I got my turn. Cherry told them what had happened before and after Johnny and I had been jumped—I think I saw a couple of tears slide down her cheeks, but I'm not sure. Her voice was sure steady even if she was crying. The judge questioned everyone carefully, but nothing real emotional or exciting happened like it does on TV. He asked Darry and Soda a little bit about Dally, I think to check our background and find out what kind of guys we hung out with. Was he a real good buddy of ours? Darry said, "Yes, sir," looking straight at the judge, not flinching; but Soda looked at me like he was sentencing me to the electric chair before he gave the same answer. I was real proud of both of them. Dally had been one of our gang and we wouldn't desert him. I thought the judge would never get around to questioning me. Man, I was scared almost stiff by the time he did. And you know what? They didn't ask me a thing about Bob's getting killed. All the judge did was ask me if I liked living with Darry, if I liked school, what kind of grades I made, and stuff like that. I couldn't figure it out then, but later I found out what the doctor had been talking to the judge about. I guess I looked as scared as I really was, because the judge grinned at me and told me to quit chewing my fingernails. That's a habit I have. Then he said I was acquitted and the whole case was closed. Just like that. Didn't even give me a chance to talk much. But that didn't bother me a lot. I didn't feel like talking anyway.

I wish I could say that everything went back to normal,

but it didn't. Especially me. I started running into things, like the door, and kept tripping over the coffee table and losing things. I always have been kind of absent-minded, but man, then, I was lucky if I got home from school with the right notebook and with both shoes on. I walked all the way home once in my stocking feet and didn't even notice it until Steve made some bright remark about it. I guess I'd left my shoes in the locker room at school, but I never did find them. And another thing, I quit eating. I used to eat like a horse, but all of a sudden I wasn't hungry. Everything tasted like baloney. I was lousing up my schoolwork, too. I didn't do too badly in math, because Darry checked over my homework in that and usually caught all my mistakes and made me do it again, but in English I really washed out. I used to make A's in English, mostly because my teacher made us do compositions all the time. I mean, I know I don't talk good English (have you ever seen a hood that did?), but I can write it good when I try. At least, I could before. Now I was lucky to get a *D* on a composition.

It bothered my English teacher, the way I was goofing up, I mean. He's a real good guy, who makes us think, and you can tell he's interested in you as a person, too. One day he told me to stay in after the rest of the class left.

"Ponyboy, I'd like to talk to you about your grades."

Man, I wished I could beat it out of there. I knew I was flunking out in that class, but golly, I couldn't help it.

"There's not much to talk about, judging from your scores. Pony, I'll give it to you straight. You're failing this class right now, but taking into consideration the circumstances, if you come up with a good semester theme, I'll pass you with a *C* grade."

"Taking into consideration the circumstances"—brother, was that ever a way to tell me he knew I was goofing up because I'd been in a lot of trouble. At least that was a roundabout way of putting it. The first week of school after the hearing had been awful. People I knew wouldn't talk to me, and people I didn't know would come right up and ask about the whole mess. Sometimes even teachers. And my history teacher—*she* acted as if she was scared of me, even though I'd never caused any trouble in her class. You can bet that made me feel real tuff.

"Yessir," I said, "I'll try. What's the theme supposed to be on?"

"Anything you think is important enough to write about. And it isn't a reference theme; I want your own ideas and your own experiences."

My first trip to the zoo. Oh, boy, oh, boy. "Yessir," I said, and got out of there as fast as I could.

At lunch hour I met Two-Bit and Steve out in the back parking lot and we drove over to a little neighborhood grocery store to buy cigarettes and Cokes and candy bars. The store was the grease hang-out and that was about all we ever had for lunch. The Socs were causing a lot of trouble in the school cafeteria—throwing silverware and stuff—and everybody tried to blame it on us greasers. We all got a big laugh out of that. Greasers rarely even eat in the cafeteria.

I was sitting on the fender of Steve's car, smoking and drinking a Pepsi while he and Two-Bit were inside talking to some girls, when a car drove up and three Socs got out. I just sat there and looked at them and took another swallow of the Pepsi. I wasn't scared. It was the oddest feeling in the world. I didn't feel *anything*—scared, mad, or anything. Just zero.

"You're the guy that killed Bob Sheldon," one of them said. "And he was a friend of ours. We don't like nobody killing our friends, especially greasers."

Big deal. I busted the end off my bottle and held on to the neck and tossed away my cigarette. "You get back into your car or you'll get split."

They looked kind of surprised, and one of them backed up.

"I mean it." I hopped off the car. "I've had about all I can take from you guys." I started toward them, holding the bottle the way Tim Shepard holds a switch—out and away from myself, in a loose but firm hold. I guess they knew I meant business, because they got into their car and drove off.

"You really would have used that bottle, wouldn't you?" Two-Bit had been watching from the store doorway. "Steve and me were backing you, but I guess we didn't need to. You'd have really cut them up, huh?"

"I guess so," I said with a sigh. I didn't see what Two-Bit was sweating about—anyone else could have done the same thing and Two-Bit wouldn't have thought about it twice.

"Ponyboy, listen, don't get tough. You're not like the rest of us and don't try to be . . ."

What was the matter with Two-Bit? I knew as well as he did that if you got tough you didn't get hurt. Get smart and nothing can touch you . . .

"What in the world are you doing?" Two-Bit's voice broke into my thoughts.

I looked up at him. "Picking up the glass."

He stared at me for a second, then grinned. "You little sonofagun," he said in a relieved voice. I didn't know what he was talking about, so I just went on picking up the glass from the bottle end and put it in a trash can. I didn't want anyone to get a flat tire.

I tried to write that theme when I got home. I really did, mostly because Darry told me to or else. I thought about writing about Dad, but I couldn't. It's going to be a long time before I can even think about my parents. A long time. I tried writing about Soda's horse, Mickey Mouse, but I couldn't get it right; it always came out sounding corny. So I started writing names across the paper. Darrel Shaynne Curtis, Jr. Soda Patrick Curtis. Ponyboy Michael Curtis. Then I drew horses all over it. *That* was going to get a good grade like all git-out.

"Hey, did the mail come in yet?" Soda slammed the door and yelled for the mail, just the way he does every day when he comes home from work. I was in the bedroom, but I knew he would throw his jacket toward the sofa and miss it, take off his shoes, and go into the kitchen for a glass of chocolate milk, because that's what he does every day of his life. He always runs around in his stocking feet—he doesn't like shoes.

Then he did a funny thing. He came in and flopped down on the bed and started smoking a cigarette. He hardly ever smokes, except when something is really bugging him or when he wants to look tough. And he doesn't have to impress us; we know he's tough. So I figured something was bothering him. "How was work?"

"Okay."

"Something wrong?"

He shook his head. I shrugged and went back to drawing horses.

Soda cooked dinner that night, and everything came out right. That was unusual, because he's always trying something different. One time we had green pancakes. Green. I can tell you one thing: if you've got a brother like Sodapop, you're never bored.

All through supper Soda was quiet, and he didn't eat much. That was really unusual. Most of the time you can't shut him up or fill him up. Darry didn't seem to notice, so I didn't say anything.

Then after supper me and Darry got into a fuss, about the fourth one we'd had that week. This one started because I hadn't done anything on that theme, and I wanted to go for a ride. It used to be that I'd just stand there and let Darry yell at me, but lately I'd been yelling right back.

"What's the sweat about my schoolwork?" I finally shouted. "I'll have to get a job as soon as I get out of school anyway. Look at Soda. He's doing okay, and he dropped out. You can just lay off!"

"You're not going to drop out. Listen, with your brains and grades you could get a scholarship, and we could put you through college. But schoolwork's not the point. You're living in a vacuum, Pony, and you're going to have to cut it out. Johnny and Dallas were our buddies, too, but you don't just stop living because you lose someone. I thought you knew that by now. You don't quit! And anytime you don't like the way I'm running things you can get out."

I went tight and cold. We never talked about Dallas or Johnny. "You'd like that, wouldn't you? You'd like me just to get out. Well, it's not that easy, is it, Soda?" But when I looked at Soda I stopped. His face was white, and when he looked at me his eyes were wide with a pained expression. I suddenly remembered Curly Shepard's face when he slipped off a telephone pole and broke his arm.

"Don't . . . Oh, you guys, why can't you . . ." He jumped up suddenly and bolted out the door. Darry and I were struck dumb. Darry picked up the envelope that Soda had dropped.

"It's the letter he wrote Sandy," Darry said without expression. "Returned unopened."

So that was what had been bugging Soda all afternoon. And I hadn't even bothered to find out. And while I was thinking about it, I realized that I never had paid much attention to Soda's problems. Darry and I just took it for granted that he didn't have any.

"When Sandy went to Florida . . . it wasn't Soda, Ponyboy. He told me he loved her, but I guess she didn't love him like he thought she did, because it wasn't him."

"You don't have to draw me a picture," I said.

"He wanted to marry her anyway, but she just left." Darry was looking at me with a puzzled expression. "Why didn't he tell you? I didn't think he'd tell Steve or Two-Bit, but I thought he told you everything."

"Maybe he tried," I said. How many times had Soda started to tell me something, only to find I was daydreaming or stuck in a book? He would always listen to me, no matter what he was doing.

"He cried every night that week you were gone," Darry

said slowly. "Both you and Sandy in the same week." He put the envelope down. "Come on, let's go after him."

We chased him clear to the park. We were gaining on him, but he had a block's head start.

"Circle around and cut him off," Darry ordered. Even out of condition I was the best runner. "I'll stay right behind him."

I headed through the trees and cut him off halfway across the park. He veered off to the right, but I caught him in a flying tackle before he'd gone more than a couple of steps. It knocked the wind out of both of us. We lay there gasping for a minute or two, and then Soda sat up and brushed the grass off his shirt.

"You should have gone out for football instead of track."

"Where did you think you were going?" I lay flat on my back and looked at him. Darry came up and dropped down beside us.

Soda shrugged. "I don't know. It's just . . . I can't stand to hear y'all fight. Sometimes . . . I just have to get out or . . . it's like I'm the middleman in a tug o' war and I'm being split in half. You dig?"

Darry gave me a startled look. Neither of us had realized what it was doing to Soda to hear us fight. I was sick and cold with shame. What he said was the truth. Darry and I did play tug of war with him, with never a thought to how much it was hurting him.

Soda was fiddling with some dead grass. "I mean, I can't take sides. It'd be a lot easier if I could, but I see both sides. Darry yells too much and tries too hard and takes everything too serious, and Ponyboy, you don't think enough, you don't realize all Darry's giving up just to give you a chance he missed out on. He could have stuck you in a home somewhere and worked his way through college. Ponyboy, I'm telling you the truth. I dropped out because I'm dumb. I really did try in school, but you saw my grades. Look, I'm happy working in a gas station with cars. You'd never be happy doing something like that. And Darry, you ought to try to understand him more, and quit bugging him about every little mistake he makes. He feels things differently than you do." He gave us a pleading look. "Golly, you two, it's bad enough having to listen to it, but when you start trying to get me to take sides . . ." Tears welled up in his eyes. "We're all we've got left. We ought to be able to stick together against everything. If we don't have each other, we don't have anything. If you don't have anything, you end up like Dallas . . . and I don't mean dead, either. I mean like he was before. And that's worse than dead. Please"—he wiped his eyes on his arm—"don't fight anymore."

Darry looked real worried. I suddenly realized that Darry was only twenty, that he wasn't so much older that he couldn't feel scared or hurt and as lost as the rest of us. I saw that I had expected Darry to do all the understanding without even trying to understand him. And he *had* given up a lot for Soda and me.

"Sure, little buddy," Darry said softly. "We're not going to fight anymore."

"Hey, Ponyboy"—Soda gave me a tearful grin—"don't you start crying, too. One bawl-baby in the family's enough."

"I'm not crying," I said. Maybe I was. I don't remember. Soda gave me a playful punch on the shoulder.

"No more fights. Okay, Ponyboy?" Darry said.

"Okay," I said. And I meant it. Darry and I would probably still have misunderstandings—we were too different not to—but no more fights. We couldn't do anything to hurt Soda. Sodapop would always be the middleman, but that didn't mean he had to keep getting pulled apart. Instead of Darry and me pulling him apart, he'd be pulling us together.

"Well," Soda said, "I'm cold. How about going home?"

"Race you," I challenged, leaping up. It was a real nice night for a race. The air was clear and cold and so clean it almost sparkled. The moon wasn't out but the stars lit up everything. It was quiet except for the sound of our feet on the cement and the dry, scraping sound of leaves blowing across the street. It was a real nice night. I guess I was still out of shape, because we all three tied. No. I guess we all just wanted to stay together.

I still didn't want to do my homework that night, though. I hunted around for a book to read, but I'd read everything in the house about fifty million times, even Darry's copy of *The Carpetbaggers*, though he'd told me I wasn't old enough to read it. I thought so too after I finished it. Finally I picked up *Gone with the Wind* and looked at it for a long time. I knew Johnny was dead. I had known it all the time, even while I was sick and pretending he wasn't. It was Johnny, not me, who had killed Bob—I knew that too. I had just thought that maybe if I played like Johnny wasn't dead it wouldn't hurt so much. The way Two-Bit, after the police had taken Dally's body away, had griped because he had lost his switchblade when they searched Dallas.

"Is that all that's bothering you, that switchblade?" a red-eyed Steve had snapped at him.

"No," Two-Bit had said with a quivering sigh, "but that's what I'm wishing was all that's bothering me."

But it still hurt anyway. You know a guy a long time, and I mean really know him, you don't get used to the idea that he's dead just overnight. Johnny was something more than a buddy to all of us. I guess he had listened to more beefs and more problems from more people than any of us. A guy that'll really listen to you, listen and care about what you're saying, is something rare. And I couldn't forget him telling me that he hadn't done enough, hadn't been out of our neighborhood all his life—and then it was too late. I took a deep breath and opened the book. A slip of paper fell out on the floor and I picked it up.

Ponyboy, I asked the nurse to give you this book so you could finish it. It was Johnny's handwriting. I went on reading, almost hearing Johnny's quiet voice. *The doctor came in a while ago but I knew anyway. I keep getting tireder and tireder. Listen, I don't mind dying now. It's worth it. It's worth saving those kids. Their lives are worth more than mine, they have more to live for. Some of their parents came by to thank me and I know it was worth it. Tell Dally it's worth it. I'm just going to miss you guys. I've been thinking about it, and that poem, that guy that wrote it, he meant you're gold when you're a kid, like green. When you're a kid everything's new, dawn. It's just when you get used to everything that it's day. Like the way you dig sunsets, Pony. That's gold. Keep that way, it's a good way to be. I want you to tell Dally to look at one. He'll probably think you're crazy, but ask for me. I don't think he's ever really seen a sunset. And don't be so bugged over being a greaser. You still have a lot of time to make yourself be what you want. There's still lots of good in the world. Tell Dally. I don't think he knows. Your buddy, Johnny.*

Tell Dally. It was too late to tell Dally. Would he have listened? I doubted it. Suddenly it wasn't only a personal thing to me. I could picture hundreds and hundreds of boys living on the wrong sides of cities, boys with black eyes who jumped at their own shadows. Hundreds of boys who maybe watched sunsets and looked at stars and ached for something better. I could see boys going down under street lights because they were mean and tough and hated the world, and it was too late to tell them that there was still good in it, and they wouldn't believe you if you did. It was too vast a problem to be just a personal thing. There should be some help, someone should tell them before it was too late. Someone should tell their side of the story, and maybe people would understand then and wouldn't be so quick to judge a boy by the amount of hair oil he wore. It was important to me. I picked up the phone book and called my English teacher.

"Mr. Syme, this is Ponyboy. That theme—how long can it be?"

"Why, uh, not less than five pages." He sounded a little surprised. I'd forgotten it was late at night.

"Can it be longer?"

"Certainly, Ponyboy, as long as you want it."

"Thanks," I said and hung up.

I sat down and picked up my pen and thought for a minute. Remembering. Remembering a handsome, dark boy with a reckless grin and a hot temper. A tough, towheaded boy with a cigarette in his mouth and a bitter grin on his hard face. Remembering—and this time it didn't hurt—a quiet, defeated-looking sixteen-year-old whose hair needed cutting badly and who had black eyes with a frightened expression to them. One week had taken all three of them. And I decided I could tell people, beginning with my English teacher. I wondered for a long time how to start that theme, how to start writing about something that was important to me. And I finally began like this: When I stepped out into the bright sunlight from the darkness of the movie house, I had only two things on my mind: Paul Newman and a ride home . . .

Speaking with S. E. Hinton...

You were a sixteen-year-old high school student in Oklahoma when you wrote *The Outsiders*. Where did you get the idea for the story?

I was actually fifteen when I first began it. It was the year I was sixteen and a junior in high school that I did the majority of the work (that was the year I made a D in creative writing). One day a friend of mine was walking home from school and these "nice" kids jumped out of a car and beat him up because they didn't like his being a greaser. This made me mad and I just went home and started pounding out a story about this boy who was beaten up while he was walking home from the movies—the beginning of *The Outsiders*. It was just something to let off steam. I didn't have any grand design. I just sat down and started writing it. I look back and I think it was totally written in my subconscious or something.

So was there a real-life Ponyboy? A real Johnny?

Ponyboy's gang was inspired by a true-life gang, the members of which were very dear to me. Later, all the gang members I hung out with were sure they were in the book—but they aren't. I guess it's because these characters are really kind of universal without losing their individuality.

How did you turn that inspiration for a story into such memorable characters?

When I write, an interesting transformation takes place. I go from thinking about my narrator to being him. A lot of Ponyboy's thoughts are my thoughts. He's probably the closest I've come to putting myself into a character. He has a lot of freedom, true-blue friends, people he loves and who love him; the things that are important to him are the things that are important to me. I think Ponyboy and Soda and Darry come out better than the rest of them because they have their love for one other.

What were you like as a teenager? Were you a greaser; a Soc?

I was a tomboy—I played football, my close friends were guys. Fortunately, I was born without the need-to-belong gene, the gene that says you have to be in a little group to feel secure.

I never wanted to be classified as anything, nor did I ever join anything for fear of losing my individuality. I didn't even realize that these guys, who were my good friends, were greasers until one day we were walking down the street and some guys came and yelled, "Greaser!" It's funny to look at people you've known all your life, to suddenly see them as everyone else sees them, with their slicked-back hair and cigarettes hanging out of their mouths and their black leather jackets, and respond, "My God, they're hoods." You know them and know they're not hoods, but they just look like hoods. I had friends on the rich side of town, too, and saw that they had their share of problems, also.

How did you pursue getting *The Outsiders* published?

When I wrote it I hadn't thought of getting it published. But at school one day I mentioned to a friend that I wrote, and her mother happened to write children's books. I gave her a copy of *The Outsiders*, and this woman showed it to a friend who had a New York agent. The agent liked it and sold it to the second publisher who read it. She has been my agent ever since. I received the contract from the publisher on graduation day!

What made you want to become a writer?

The major influence on my writing has been my reading. When I was young, I read everything, including cereal boxes and coffee labels. Reading taught me sentence structure, paragraphing, how to build a chapter. Strangely enough, it never taught me spelling.

I have always loved to write, almost as much as I love to read. I began goofing around with a typewriter when I was about twelve. I've always written about things that interest me, so my first years of writing (grades three through ten), I wrote about cowboys and horses. I wanted to be a cowboy and have a horse.

Writing is easy for me because I never begin to write unless I have something to say. I'm a character writer. Some writers are plot writers. . . . I have to begin with people. I always know my characters, exactly what they look like, their birthdays, what they like for breakfast. It doesn't matter if these things appear in the book. I still have to know. I get ideas for characters from real people, but overall they are fictional; my characters exist only in my head.

What books and authors inspire and influence you?

Well, as an adult, I can pick out a lot of authors who have influenced me. My favorite authors are Jane Austen, Mary Renault, F. Scott Fitzgerald, and Shirley Jackson. My favorite books are *The Haunting of Hill House*, *Fire from Heaven*, *Emma*, and *Tender Is the Night*. I like Kurt Vonnegut Jr.'s novels, but not his short stories, and the other way around for J. D. Salinger.

But people want to know your childhood influences,

and I'll have to say just books in general. I loved to read, and as soon as I learned how I was reading everything I could get my hands on. I was a horse nut, and *Peanuts the Pony* was the first book I ever checked out of the library. I still remember that book. The act of reading was so pleasurable for me. For an introverted kid, it's a means of communication, because you interact with the author even if you aren't sitting there conversing with her.

Why do you use your initials instead of your full name?

My publisher was afraid that the reviewers would assume a girl couldn't write a book like *The Outsiders*. Later, when my books became popular, I found I liked the privacy of having a "public" name and a private one, so it has worked out fine.

When it was first published, the realism of *The Outsiders* shocked a lot of reviewers, but readers embraced the book. Did that surprise you?

No, I was pleased that people were shocked when *The Outsiders* came out. One of my reasons for writing it was that I wanted something realistic to be written about teenagers. At that time realistic teenage fiction didn't exist. If you didn't want to read *Mary Jane Goes to the Prom* and you were through with horse books, there was nothing to read. I just wanted to write something that dealt with what I saw kids really doing.

Why do you think the book has remained so popular through the years?

Every teenager feels that adults have no idea what's going on. That's exactly the way I felt when I wrote *The Outsiders*. Even today, the concept of the in-group and the out-group remains the same. The kids say, "Okay, this is like the Preppies and the Punks," or whatever they call themselves. The uniforms change, and the names of the groups change, but kids really grasp how similar their situations are to Ponyboy's.

Some portions were quoted from *"The Outsiders* Conference & Readers Meet Author" from University of Utah's *Top of the News*, November 1968; "S. E. Hinton: On Writing and *Tex"* in Notes from Delacorte Press, Winter 1979/Spring 1980; "S. E. Hinton on Becoming a Writer" from teachers@random; "The Insider Outsider" in *Interview*, July 1999; and "Autobiographical Sketch" from the Educational Paperback Association.

Turn the page for a discussion guide
to S. E. Hinton's
THE OUTSIDERS

THE OUTSIDERS
Discussion Guide

1.   One of the primary themes in *The Outsiders* is the struggle between the greasers and the Socs (pronounced SOSH-es). Describe each group. What is the main source of tension between the two groups? Are the two groups really so different?

2.   What other works have you read that adopt a similar thematic structure?

3.   Have you ever felt like an outsider? Why did you feel that way, and how did it make you feel?

4.   Do you think that different groups of people are treated differently? If so, how? If not, why not?

5.   Imagine that you were a character in the book. Would you be associated with the greasers or the Socs? Why?

6.   Discuss the various attitudes toward fighting found in *The Outsiders*. Which attitudes do you agree with? Which attitudes do you disagree with? Do you feel that violence can ever be justified?

7.   Who is the narrator of *The Outsiders*? What point of view is it told in? What effect do you think this has on the story?

8. How do Ponyboy's relationships with Darry and Sodapop differ? Explain. Do you think Darry loves Ponyboy? Why does he treat Ponyboy the way he does?

9. Johnny is portrayed as being particularly quiet and sensitive. Why do you think he is this way? How do the other greasers treat him?

10. Why is the "gang" so important to Johnny? How is his family situation different from that of Ponyboy and his brothers?

11. Dallas is portrayed as a particularly tough character. What makes Ponyboy admire him? Is Dally redeemed by his love and concern for Johnny?

12. Ponyboy says, "I lie to myself all the time." What do you think he means by this? And why do you think he does it? Do you ever lie to yourself? Why?

13. What does Cherry tell Ponyboy is the difference between the Socs and the greasers? How does this differ from Ponyboy's perspective on the situation?

14. Ponyboy says, "Johnny and I understood each other without saying anything." What does he mean by this statement? Have you ever had a relationship with someone who you understood, or who understood you, without having to say anything?

15. When and how did Pony's parents die? How were his and his brothers' lives changed by this?

16. How do Johnny's prior experiences with the Socs affect his behavior in the park? Does the fact that he was defending his friend's life justify his actions? Why or why not?

17. What is your definition of a hero? Do you think that Johnny, Ponyboy, and Dallas are heroes? Explain.

18. Ponyboy says that he would rather have someone's hate than their pity. Why do you think he says this?

19. Ponyboy says, "Johnny didn't have anything to do with Bob's getting killed." What do you think he means by this? Does he believe that this is true?

20. Johnny leaves the copy of *Gone with the Wind* to Ponyboy. Why is this significant? How does it illustrate their friendship?

21. Examine Robert Frost's poem "Nothing Gold Can Stay." What do you think the poem is saying? How does this apply to the characters in the novel? What does Johnny mean when he tells Pony to "stay gold"?

22. Do you think it is obvious that the novel was written when the author was only sixteen years old? Support your answer with details from the book.

Turn the page to read an excerpt from
THAT WAS THEN, THIS IS NOW

1

Mark and me went down to the bar/pool hall about
two or three blocks from where we lived with the sole
intention of making some money. We'd done that before. I was a really good pool player, especially for
being just sixteen years old, and, what's more, I look
like a baby-faced kid who wouldn't know one ball
from another. This, and the way Mark set me up,
helped me hustle a lot of pool games. The bad deal is,
it's against the law to be in this pool hall if you're
under age, because of the adjoining bar. The good
deal is, the bartender and owner was a good friend of
mine, being the older brother of this chick I used to
like. When this chick and me broke up, I still stayed
friends with her brother, which is unusual in cases like
that. Charlie, the bartender, was just twenty-two, but
he had a tough reputation and kept order real good.
We lived in kind of a rough part of town and some
pretty wild things went on in Charlie's Bar.

I looked around for a plainclothes cop when we

went in—I can always tell a cop—but didn't find one, so I went up to the bar and hopped on a barstool

"Give me a beer," I said, and Charlie, who was cleaning glasses just like every bartender you ever see, gave me a dirty look instead. "O.K.," I said brightly, "a Coke."

"Your credit ain't so hot, Bryon," Charlie said. "You got cash?"

"A dime—for cryin' out loud! Can't you let me charge a dime Coke?"

"Cokes are fifteen cents, and you already got three dollars worth of Cokes charged here, and if you don't pay up this month I'll have to beat it out of you." He said this real friendly-like, but he meant it. We were friends, but Charlie was a businessman too.

"I'll pay up," I assured him. "Don't worry."

Charlie gave me a lopsided grin. "I ain't worried, kid. You're the one who should be worried."

I was, to tell the truth. Charlie was a big, tough guy so a three-dollar beating up was something to worry about.

"Hey, Mark," Charlie called, "there ain't nobody here to hustle."

Mark, who had been scouting out the two guys playing pool, came up and sat down next to me. "Yeah, that's the truth."

"It's just as well," Charlie said. "You guys are going to get in real bad trouble one of these days. Some guy's going to get hacked off when he finds out what you're doin', and you're gonna get a pool stick rammed down your throats."

"No we ain't," Mark said. "Give me a Coke, Charlie."

"We don't have any credit," I said glumly.

Mark stared at Charlie disbelievingly. "You got to be kiddin'. Man, when did we ever not pay our bill?"

"Last month."

"You said you'd add it on to this month's. That's what you said. So I don't see why you can't add twenty cents to that."

"Thirty cents," corrected Charlie. "And, like I just told Bryon, if I don't get that money pretty soon, I'm going to take it out of a couple of hides."

"I'll get you the money tomorrow if you give us the Cokes right now."

"O.K." Charlie gave in to Mark. Almost everybody does. It was a gift he had, a gift for getting away with things. He could talk anyone into anything. "But if I don't get the money by tomorrow, I'll come looking for you."

I got chilled. I had heard Charlie say that to another guy once. I also saw the guy after Charlie found him. But if Mark said he'd have three dollars by tomorrow, he'd have it.

"Speaking of looking for you," Charlie continued, "the true flower child was in here asking for you."

"M&M?" Mark asked. "What did he want?"

"How would I know? Man, that is a weird kid. Nice guy, but weird."

"Yeah," Mark said. "I guess it would be hard to be a hippie in a hood's part of town."

"Speak for yourself, man," Charlie said. "This part of town don't make nobody a hood."

"You're right," Mark said. "But I really sounded profound there for a minute, huh?"

Charlie just gave him a funny look and got us the Cokes. It was later in the evening now, and some more customers came in, so Charlie quit talking to us. It got pretty busy.

"Where are you gonna get three dollars?" I asked Mark.

He finished off his Coke. "I don't know."

That bugged the heck out of me. Mark was always pulling stunts like that. I ought to know; Mark had lived at my house ever since I was ten and he was nine and his parents shot each other in a drunken argument and my old lady felt sorry for him and took him home to live with us. My mother wanted a hundred kids and could have only one, so until she got hold of Mark she had to be content feeding every stray cat that came along. There was no telling how many kids she might have picked up along the line if she could have afforded more than two—me and Mark.

I had been friends with Mark long before he came

to live with us. He had lived down the street and it seemed to me that we had always been together. We had never had a fight. We had never even had an argument. In looks, we were complete opposites: I'm a big guy, dark hair and eyes—the kind who looks like a Saint Bernard puppy, which I don't mind as most chicks cannot resist a Saint Bernard puppy. Mark was small and compact, with strange golden eyes and hair to match and a grin like a friendly lion. He was much stronger than he looked—he could tie me in arm wrestling. He was my best friend and we were like brothers.

"Let's go look for M&M," Mark said abruptly and we left. It was dark outside and seemed a little chilly. This was probably because school had just started, and it always seems like fall when school starts, even if it's hot. Charlie's Bar was on a real crummy street with a lot of other bars whose bartenders kicked us out when we strolled in, a movie house, a drugstore, and a second-hand clothes store that always had a sign in the window saying "We Buy Almost Anything"—and from the looks of their clothes, they did. When my old lady went into the hospital, we got so low on money that I bought some clothes there. It's pretty lousy, buying used clothes.

We found M&M in the drugstore reading *Newsweek,* which shows what a weird kid he was since there were plenty of skin mags and things to read. A little kid like him shouldn't be reading that junk, I know, but he should at least want to.

"Hey, Charlie said you was lookin' for us," Mark greeted him.

M&M looked up at him. "Yeah. How you guys doin'?"

M&M was the most serious guy I knew. He always had this wide-eyed, intent, trusting look on his face, but sometimes he smiled, and when he did it was really great. He was an awful nice kid even if he was a little strange. He had big gray eyes—the kind you see on war-orphan posters—and charcoal-colored hair down past his ears and down to his eyebrows. He probably would have grown a beard except thirteen was too young for it. He always wore an old Army jacket that was too big for him and went barefoot even after it started getting cold. Then his father got fed up with it and M&M got a pair of moccasins. He had a metal peace symbol hanging around his neck on a piece of rawhide string, and he got his nickname from his addiction to M&M's, the kind of chocolate candy that melts in your mouth and not in your hand. For years I'd never seen M&M without a bag of that candy. I don't know how he ate those things all day long, day after day. If I did that, my face would break out like nothing you've ever seen.

"You want an M&M?" He held out a bag toward us. I shook my head, but Mark took one, just to be polite, since he didn't like sweet stuff. "You wanted to see us for something?" Mark reminded him.

"Yeah, I did, but I forgot what for." He was like that. Real absent-minded. "My sister's home," he added as an afterthought.

"No kiddin'?" asked Mark tactfully, thumbing through a *Playboy*. "Which one?"

M&M had a million brothers and sisters, most of them younger. They all looked alike and it was really funny to see him out somewhere with four or five little carbon copies—with dark hair and big serious eyes—hanging all over him. If I had to be a baby-sitter day and night, I'd lose my temper and kill one of those brats, but then, M&M never lost his temper.

"My older sister, Cathy. You know."

"Yeah, I remember," I said, only I didn't remember too well. "Where's she been?"

"She went to a private school last year and this summer. She's been staying with my aunt. She had to come home, though, because she ran out of money. She paid for it all with her own bread."

"Must be smart," I said. I couldn't remember what she looked like; I had never paid any attention to her. "She as smart as you?"

"No," M&M said, still reading. He wasn't bragging, he was telling the truth. He was a very honest kid.

"Let's go over to the bowling alley," Mark suggested. The drugstore wasn't exactly jumping with action. It was a school night and nobody was hanging around. "You come too, M&M."

It was a long walk to the bowling alley, and I wished for the hundredth time I had a car. I had to walk everywhere I went. As if he'd read my mind, which he was in the habit of doing, Mark said, "I could hot-wire us a car."

"That's a bad thing to do," M&M said. "Taking something that doesn't belong to you."

"It ain't stealin'," Mark said. "It's borrowin'."

"Yeah, well, you're on probation now for 'borrowing,' so I don't think it's such a great idea," I said.

Mark could hot-wire anything, and ever since he was twelve years old he had hot-wired cars and driven them. He had never had an accident, but he finally got caught at it, so now once a week he had to go downtown on his school lunch hour to see his probation officer and tell him how he was never going to steal cars any more. I had been worried at first, afraid they were going to take Mark and put him in a boys' home since he wasn't really my brother and didn't have a family. I was worried about Mark being locked up. I didn't need to. Mark always came through everything untouched, unworried, unaffected.

"O.K." Mark shrugged. "Don't get shook, Bryon."

"Bryon," M&M said suddenly, "were you named after the lord?"

"What?" I said, stunned. For a minute I thought he meant God.

"Lord Bryon, were you named after him?"

The poor kid had *Byron* and *Bryon* mixed up. I decided to string him along. "Yeah, I was."

"Was there a Lord Bryon?" Mark said. "Hey, that's cool." He paused. "I guess it's cool. What'd this guy do, anyway?"

"Can't tell you in front of the kid," I answered.

M&M shook his head. "He wrote poetry. He wrote long, old poems. You ought to write poetry, just to keep up the tradition of the Bryons."

"You ought to keep your mouth shut," I replied, "before I keep up the tradition of punching wise guys in the mouth."

M&M looked up at me, and I realized from his hurt, puzzled look that he hadn't been trying to be smart. So I punched him on the shoulder and said, "O.K., I'll write poetry. How's this?"—and I recited a dirty limerick I'd heard somewhere. It made him laugh and turn red at the same time. Mark thought I had made it up, and said, "Hey, that was pretty good. Can you just pop them off like that?"

I only shrugged and said, "Sometimes," because then I'd take credit whether or not it was really due me. I was like that. I'd also lie if I really thought I could get away with it, especially to girls. Like telling them I loved them and junk, when I didn't. I had a rep as a lady-killer—a hustler. I kept up the old Lord Byron tradition in one way. Sometimes I'd get to feeling bad thinking about how rotten I treated some of these

17

chicks, but most of the time it didn't even bother me.

"M&M, old buddy," Mark was saying, putting his arm across M&M's shoulders, "I was wondering if you might be able to loan your best friend some money."

"You ain't my best friend," M&M said with that disarming honesty, "but how much do you want?"

"Three bucks."

"I got fifty cents." M&M reached into his jeans pocket and pulled out a couple of quarters. "Here."

"Forget it," I said. Me and Mark looked at each other and shook our heads. M&M was unbelievable.

"It's O.K. I'll get fifty cents again next week, for baby-sitting."

"Is that all you get paid for watching all those kids? Fifty cents?" I couldn't get over it. Fifty cents a week?

"I think it's enough. I don't mind taking care of the kids. Who's going to do it if I don't. Both my parents work, so they can't do it. Anyway, I like my family. When I get married I'm going to have at least nine or ten kids."

"There goes the population explosion," Mark said.

"Well, now that your sister's home she can do a lot of the baby-sitting," I said, trying to be helpful. M&M could tell we thought he was crazy.

"Cathy's got a job after school; she can't help. I don't know what I have to do to convince you that I don't mind it."

"O.K., O.K., I'm convinced." I was also tired of the

subject and I had got to worrying about how we were going to get three dollars before tomorrow. Charlie didn't get his rough rep or his bar by being nice to people, especially ones who couldn't pay their bills.

By the time we got to the bowling alley it was ten o'clock. There weren't many people there. Mark and I watched a few games while M&M stared into a package of M&M's. I finally got bugged about it and asked him what in the Sam Hill was he doing.

"Take a look." He handed me the package, which was open at the top. "Put it right up to your eye."

I did, and all I saw was a bunch of candy.

"It's beautiful, ain't it?" asked M&M. "I mean, look at all the different colors."

"Yeah," I agreed, thinking, If I didn't know this kid better I'd say he was high.

"Let me look," said Mark, so I handed him the package. "Hey, this is groovy. Look at all the colors." He gave the candy back to M&M, looked at me, and shrugged.

M&M got up. "I gotta go home now. I'll see you guys later."

"We just got here," Mark objected.

"Yeah, well, I just came along for the walk, and now I gotta go home."

I watched him leave. "The kid's weird," I said. "That's all there is to it."

Mark lit up a cigarette, our last one, so we had to

pass it back and forth. "I know, but I still get a kick out of him. Come on, let's go catch up with him. There ain't nothin' to do around here."

Outside I spotted M&M at the corner. There were three guys trailing him. When you see something like that around here you know right away somebody is about to get jumped. In this case, it was M&M.

"Come on," Mark said, and we cut through an alley so as to come up behind those guys.

Three against three. The odds would have been even except that M&M was one of those nonviolent types who practiced what he preached, and me and Mark weren't carrying weapons. We slowed down to a walk when we came to the end of the alley. I could hear the voices of the three guys who were following M&M, and I recognized one of them.

"Hey, flower child, turn around." They were taunting him, but M&M just kept right on moving.

"It's Shepard," Mark whispered to me. We were waiting at the end of the alley for them to come by. They didn't. They must have had M&M up against the wall. We could hear them.

"Hey, hippie, don't you answer when you're spoken to? That ain't nice."

"Curly, why don't you leave me alone?" M&M sounded very patient. I moved over to the other side of the alley just in time to see Curly pull out a switchblade and reach over and cut through the rawhide string on M&M's peace medal. It fell to the ground.

20

M&M reached down to pick it up, and Curly brought his knee up sharply and hit M&M in the face.

Me and Mark looked at each other, and Mark flashed me a grin. We both liked fights. We ran out and jumped on them, and the one we didn't get took off, which was a wise thing for him to do. Since we had surprised them, it wasn't too hard to get them pinned. I had Curly Shepard in a stranglehold with one arm twisted behind his back, while Mark had the other guy pinned on the ground.

"How'd you like a broken arm, Shepard?" I said through gritted teeth, careful not to loosen my grip. His switchblade had fallen on the sidewalk, but I didn't know what all he might be carrying. He liked to play rough.

"O.K., you proved your point. Let us go, Douglas." Curly said a few more things that I'm not going to repeat. He must have figured out who it was twisting his arm when he saw Mark. Me and Mark were always together. Curly had a special grudge against me anyway. I used to go with his sister; she says she broke up with me, which was the truth, but I was spreading it around that I broke up with her and was giving all kinds of cool reasons. Curly was a little dumb—he belonged to a gang led by his brother Tim and known as the Shepard Gang. Really original. Tim was all right—at least he had a few brains—but I considered Curly a dumb hood. "Look, we didn't hurt him."

That was a lie, because M&M was sitting there

against the wall and already his cheek was swelling up and turning purple. He was trying to tie the ends of the rawhide string together and his hands were shaking.

"Let them go," said M&M. "I'm O.K."

I gave Curly's arm an extra twist for good measure and then gave him a shove that almost sent him sprawling. Mark let the other guy up, but when he was almost to his feet, Mark gave him a good swift kick. They left, cussing us out, partly in English and partly in sign language.

Mark was helping M&M up. "Come on, kid," he said easily. "Let's get you home."

The whole side of M&M's face was bruised, but he gave us one of his rare, wistful grins. "Thanks, you guys."

Mark suddenly laughed. "Hey, look what I got." He waved three one-dollar bills at me.

"Where did you get that?" I asked, although I knew good and well where he got it. Mark was very quick; nobody had to teach him how to hot-wire a car—or to pick a pocket.

"It was a donation," Mark said seriously, "for the Cause."

This was an old joke, but M&M fell for it. "What cause?"

" 'Cause we owe it to Charlie," Mark said, and M&M almost laughed, but instead winced with pain. I was really feeling good. I could quit worrying about Charlie's beating us up.

Mark suddenly poked me. "You still in the mood for a little action?"

"Sure," I said. Mark motioned toward the next intersection. There was a black guy standing there, waiting for the light to change. "We could jump him," Mark said, but suddenly M&M spoke up.

"You make me sick! You just rescued me from some guys who were going to beat me up because I'm different from them, and now you're going to beat up someone because he's different from you. You think I'm weird—well, you're the weird ones."

Both Mark and I had stopped walking and were staring at M&M. He was really shook up. He was crying. I couldn't have been more stunned if he had begun to dissolve. You don't see guys crying around here, not unless they have a lot better reason than M&M had. He suddenly took off, running, not looking back. I started to take a few steps after him, but Mark caught me by the arm. "Leave him alone," Mark said. "He's just all uptight from getting jumped."

"Yeah," I said. That made sense. That had happened to me before, and I could remember how scared it could get you. Besides, M&M was only a kid, just turned thirteen.

Mark picked something up off the ground. It was M&M's peace medal. It must have dropped off when

M&M started running. He hadn't tied the ends of the string together very well.

"Remind me to tell him I have this," Mark said, stuffing the medal and the string in his pocket. "Let's stop by and give this three bucks to Charlie before I buy some cigarettes with it."

"O.K.," I said. I didn't feel quite as good as I had before. I was thinking about what M&M had said about beating up people because they were different. There was a lot of truth to that. The rich kids in town used to drive around over in our part of the city and look for people to beat up. Then a year or so ago a couple of kids got killed in that mess and the fad slowly died out. But there were still gang fights around here and social-club rumbles, and things like Shepard's jumping M&M happened every day. I didn't mind it much, unless I was the one getting mugged. I liked fights.

"Come on," Mark called, "maybe there's somebody to hustle in Charlie's." I grinned and ran to catch up with him. Mark was my best buddy and I loved him like a brother.

S. E. HINTON's career as an author began while she was still a student at Will Rogers High School in Tulsa, Oklahoma. Disturbed by the clashes of the two gangs in her high school, the greasers and the Socs, Hinton wrote *The Outsiders*, an honest, sometimes shocking novel told from the point of view of a fourteen-year-old greaser named Ponyboy Curtis.

The Outsiders was published during Hinton's freshman year at the University of Tulsa, and was an immediate sensation. Today, with more than fourteen million copies in print, the book is the bestselling young adult novel of all time. The book was also made into a film in 1983, directed by Francis Ford Coppola and featuring budding young stars Tom Cruise, Matt Dillon, and Rob Lowe.

The Outsiders brought with it publicity and fame. S. E. Hinton became known as "The Voice of the Youth." This overnight success also brought a lot of pressure, resulting in a three-year-long writer's block. Her boyfriend (now husband) eventually helped break this block by suggesting she write two pages a day before going anywhere. This ultimately led to her second novel, *That Was Then, This Is Now*. Ms. Hinton went on to write several other novels, including *Rumble Fish* and *Tex*.

In 1988 she was awarded the first annual Margaret A. Edwards Award, given in honor of "an author whose book or books, over a period of time, have been accepted by young adults as an authentic voice that continues to illuminate their experiences and emotions, giving insight into their lives."

S. E. Hinton still lives in Oklahoma with her husband and son, where she enjoys writing, riding horses, and taking courses at the university.